Christopher Michel

JOHN JAY OSBORN is a law professor who writes novels. When two of them, *The Paper Chase* and *The Associates*, were made into television shows, he went to work in Hollywood. He came to his senses and returned to ~~being a~~ law professor who writes novels ~~He lives with~~ his family in San Franci~~sco~~

ALSO BY JOHN JAY OSBORN

The Paper Chase
The Only Thing I've Done Wrong
The Associates
The Man Who Owned New York
The California Coast

Additional Praise for *Listen to the Marriage*

"[A] slim, swift-reading novel . . . The book's page-turning drama . . . is driven by a race: Will the characters learn enough in time to stay together?"
—Lou Fancher, *The Mercury News*

"[*Listen to the Marriage*] is a slim yet immersive story."
—Jessica Zack, *San Francisco Chronicle*

"A beneficial read for any couple in a long-term relationship or marriage. The blush of the honeymoon may be long over, and despite hurt and pain—or if there is none—this novel can be a guide to discover if their partnership is viable or to help strengthen it."
—Nancy Carty Lepri, *New York Journal of Books*

"Excellent . . . Readers with relationship experience will find here the realistic issues of compromise, sacrifice, communication, and also much that is new in terms of how to nurture a relationship . . . Deeply engaging and insightful, [*Listen to the Marriage*] is enthusiastically recommended for anyone who has ever been (or wishes to be) married."
—Patrick Sullivan, *Library Journal*

"A nuanced portrait of what makes a marriage work . . . It takes dedication, self-reflection, and lots and lots of communication . . . Emotionally intelligent and deeply felt."
—*Publishers Weekly*

"This surprisingly dramatic, voyeuristic novel is based in part on the author's own experiences, lending it an intimate, authentic feel."
—*Good Housekeeping*

john jay osborn

Listen to the
Marriage

PICADOR

FARRAR,
STRAUS
AND
GIROUX

New York

LISTEN TO THE MARRIAGE. Copyright © 2018 by John Jay Osborn. All rights reserved. Printed in the United States of America. For information, address Picador, 120 Broadway, New York, N.Y. 10271.

picadorusa.com • instagram.com/picador
twitter.com/picadorusa • facebook.com/picadorusa

Picador® is a U.S. registered trademark and is used by Macmillan Publishing Group, LLC, under license from Pan Books Limited.

For book club information, please visit facebook.com/picadorbookclub or email marketing@picadorusa.com.

Designed by Richard Oriolo

The Library of Congress has cataloged
the Farrar, Straus and Giroux edition as follows:

Names: Osborn, John Jay, author.
Title: Listen to the marriage / John Jay Osborn.
Description: First edition. | New York : Farrar, Straus and Giroux, 2018.
Identifiers: LCCN 2018002525 | ISBN 9780374192020 (hardcover) | ISBN 9780374718787 (ebook)
Classification: LCC PS3565.S38 L57 2018 | DDC 813/.54—dc23
LC record available at https://lccn.loc.gov/2018002525

Picador Paperback 978-1-250-23476-6

Our books may be purchased in bulk for promotional, educational, or business use. Please contact your local bookseller or the Macmillan Corporate and Premium Sales Department at 1-800-221-7945, extension 5442, or by email at MacmillanSpecialMarkets@macmillan.com.

First published by Farrar, Straus and Giroux

First Picador Edition: October 2019

10 9 8 7 6 5 4 3 2 1

To Marilyn Harris Kriegel and
Frederick Schieffelin Osborn

Listen to the Marriage

LITERARY SELECTIONS DESIGNED TO

GARCIA STREET BOOKS
SANTA FE, NEW MEXICO

SURPRISE, INSPIRE AND DELIGHT

1.

"Is there anything practical that needs to be addressed right now?" Sandy asked.

Like a student, Gretchen raised her hand.

It had been a long time since one of the couples who came to Sandy had raised a hand before speaking.

"Okay, Gretchen," Sandy said. "What's going on?"

"I'm worried about money," Gretchen said. "Since I moved out, I've had to rent an apartment, furnish it, pay for new childcare."

"How much money do you have?" Sandy asked.

"I don't know," Gretchen said. "In my checking account right now, I have three thousand dollars. The rest of our money? Steve handles it."

Sandy turned to Steve, Gretchen's husband. He was slumped in the chair across from Gretchen.

"So, Steve, what is the money situation?" Sandy asked.

"I just became a full partner at Simpson Weaver," Steve said. "I had a chance to buy into the partnership fund. It took all of our uncommitted resources."

"Are you saying that you and Gretchen have no money?" Sandy asked.

"Of course we have money," Steve said. "I think there is about twenty thousand dollars in our Vanguard money market fund. It's all going to work out. Now that I'm a partner, I can borrow as much money as I need."

You had to buy into the partnership fund, but then you can borrow as much as you want? Sandy thought.

"As I understand it, you guys just sold a house in Ross," Sandy said. "Where's the money from that?"

"We closed escrow this morning," Steve said. "I have a check for two hundred thousand dollars."

Sandy's mother had been a legendary real estate maven. In fact, this office was in one of her mother's buildings. Sandy knew something about real estate.

"You sold a house in Ross, and the total cash you got was only two hundred thousand dollars?" Sandy said.

"I had to mortgage the house," Steve said. "I took out every penny I could."

"To buy into the partnership fund?" Sandy said evenly.

"It sounds crazy," Steve said. "But that's the way it works."

He leaned forward in his chair.

"You think this is nuts, don't you? You think I've been scamming Gretchen or something," Steve said.

"I've known you for about half an hour," Sandy said. "I have no idea what you're doing to Gretchen. All I know is that Gretchen is worried about money."

"So we can split the money from the house," Steve said.

"Are you worried about money?" Sandy asked Steve.

"Not really," he said. "Soon I'll have my first partnership draw."

"And you can borrow as much as you want until then?" Sandy asked.

"Yes, sure," Steve said.

"I think you should give the two hundred thousand dollars from the house to Gretchen," Sandy said.

Sandy saw it hit him. He almost lashed out. Somehow he got control of himself.

"That's interesting," Steve said deliberately, cautiously. Sandy waited for more.

"The whole two hundred thousand dollars?" Steve said.

"Yes," Sandy said. "All of it. Gretchen has taken a huge step, moving out on her own with the kids. On top of everything else, do you want her worried about money?"

That's right, Steve, Sandy was saying. She left you, but I want you to give her the whole two hundred thousand dollars. Can you see why?

"But half of it belongs to Steve," Gretchen said. She looked so earnest, and so blond, blue-eyed, so all-American. It was like, What am I doing here? This isn't my movie.

"What do you mean, half of it belongs to Steve?" Sandy asked.

"If we got divorced, half would be his," Gretchen said.

"Do you want to get divorced?" Sandy asked.

"I don't know," Gretchen said slowly. "Probably, but we have two children."

"I'm a marriage therapist," Sandy said. "Frankly, I don't care what the law says. You can find a lawyer to explain that to you. What I see is that you're worried about money. I think two hundred thousand dollars would take your worry about money off the table, at least for the time being. You told me that you're primarily responsible for the kids plus you're working full-time. I think you're going to need all kinds of help. Do you want to be worried about money on top of everything else?"

Gretchen lit up. "You really think I should have the whole two hundred thousand?" she said.

"Yes," Sandy said.

She turned to look at Steve. His shirt was pressed, his shoes were shined, his pants had a neat crease. But his brown eyes had deep circles under them, and his hands shook. He was trying to hold himself together.

"What do you think, Steve?" Sandy asked.

"I think most guys would say: My wife is about to divorce me, and the marriage counselor wants me to give my wife all of the cash from the house? When legally one-half belongs to me? Why would I do that?" Steve said. "That's what most guys would say."

"That is what most guys would say," Sandy said. "What about you?"

Amazingly, he smiled.

"When you said the whole two hundred thousand should go to Gretchen, I was like, Wow." Steve paused. "I was like: What is going on here? I felt ambushed. I thought, While we're trying to decide whether to get a divorce or not, shouldn't everything be frozen in place?"

The last thing Sandy believed was that everything should be frozen in place.

"Do you want a divorce?" Sandy asked.

Steve didn't answer. What was he feeling? Sandy wondered if he could talk about it. She asked: "How are you feeling, Steve?"

"How I'm feeling?" It was as if this were a question he had not allowed himself to consider.

"My wife has moved out with the kids. I just made

partner at a private equity firm but I feel worse than I've ever felt in my life. I haven't slept for weeks."

He stopped talking, looked at Gretchen sitting across from him. It was as if he wanted to take stock. Who was she? He didn't know anymore.

She's a beautiful, smart ice princess and you really fucked this up, Sandy thought.

Would Sandy take them on? She wasn't sure. Where were the brooding, melancholy artists? She never saw them. Was Steve brooding? Brooding, introspective, willing to change? Was it possible that he could change? Did he write poetry late at night? Did he paint watercolors? Did he realize how beautiful it was here, in this city, at this time of year?

She looked over at Gretchen. And could you change? It might actually be harder for you, princess.

Steve was looking around the office, the desk in the corner, the Scandinavian armchairs, and behind them, the big green Victorian armchair. Was he thinking it was out of place in the office? The two windows showing the top of the pepper tree outside. Sandy realized that Steve hadn't noticed his surroundings, where he was, as he stumbled in, having trouble just getting to his chair. Now he was centering himself.

"Steve?" Sandy said.

"Sorry," he said. "So why would I give Gretchen the half of the money that belongs to me? Why should I do that?"

"Because she's worried about money," Sandy said.

"I don't want to get divorced," Steve said quietly, finally answering Sandy's question.

"But you are teetering on the edge of it," Sandy said. "What you've been doing hasn't worked. You should try something new. Something you would never do. Something that seems counterintuitive. Why not? What do you have to lose?"

"Money," Steve said.

Wrong answer, Steve. Sandy just looked at him: Steve, it is all on the line right now. Do you get that?

"Try something counterintuitive?" Steve said after a moment.

"Why not?" Sandy said.

He was still clinging by his fingertips to what most guys thought. Let go, Steve, Sandy thought. He looked away, into the middle distance.

"I'm tired," Steve said.

"I know," Sandy said. Let go, you've been holding on too long, she thought.

He did. Sandy sensed him let go of the guys and the advice that never works and fall into the unknown.

"Okay," Steve said. "Let's try counterintuitive."

He reached into his jacket pocket and pulled out an envelope.

"I happen to have the check with me."

He opened the envelope, took out a check. He took the Montblanc pen from his shirt pocket and endorsed the check. He handed it to Gretchen. She took it. Two hundred thousand dollars.

"Thank you," she said.

Sandy thought these were probably the first kind words Steve had heard from Gretchen in a long time. *Thank you*. See, Steve, Sandy thought, you tried something counterintuitive and already it's working.

Yes, she would take them on.

2.

Sandy always saw her couples for individual sessions at the beginning.

Two days later, when Gretchen came in alone, she looked exhausted, just dead tired. And she was late too, though just by a few minutes. She ran up the stairs to Sandy's second-floor office.

"I'm sorry I'm late," she said. She went to the chair she'd sat in before. "Thank God you have the little parking lot."

She put her brown leather bag on the floor next to her chair. She breathed deeply a few times.

"This is a wonderful building," she said. "I saw the bronze plaque on the wall near the stairs. You thank your mother for giving you the building."

My mother put up that plaque, Sandy remembered.

"Thank you," Sandy said. "What's up? You look exhausted."

It brought Gretchen up short. She snapped into the moment.

"I am," Gretchen said. "Last night, I stayed up until two in the morning grading papers, and then I had to get up with the kids and get them to school on Dolores and then I drive to Fillmore to see you, then later, I need to get back across town to teach class at USF, then back to Dolores to pick up the kids. I don't know, Sandy."

"What don't you know?" Sandy asked.

"If one little thing goes wrong, if school calls because one of the kids is sick, the whole house of cards tumbles," Gretchen said.

"Where does Steve fit into all of this?" Sandy asked.

"He picks the kids up at school two days a week, and every other weekend he has them," Gretchen said.

"So if one of the kids got sick, and you had to teach, why wouldn't you ask Steve to take over?" Sandy asked.

"I don't want to ask Steve for anything," Gretchen said

evenly. "I don't even like the fact that he has the children two afternoons a week."

"We should talk about that," Sandy said. "But maybe not right now. Why don't you hire someone to help you out with the kids?"

"I don't want them to feel abandoned by me," Gretchen said. "They're already upset that Steve and I aren't together."

Sandy shook her head.

"You're a professor at a university that must have a thousand talented students who need part-time jobs. Your kids might like to spend an afternoon with one of them, rather than with their exhausted mother, who can barely keep her eyes open because she was up all night grading papers," Sandy said.

There was more, Sandy knew.

"But it wasn't just grading papers, was it?" Sandy said.

"I was also on the phone for an hour or so," Gretchen said quietly.

"This would be with some guy, right?"

"Yes."

"Tell me about it," Sandy said.

"I'm embarrassed," Gretchen said slowly.

"You'll get over it," Sandy said. She smiled at Gretchen. And you will, she thought.

Gretchen nodded.

"So right after I got tenure, I went to a conference about

Dickens and his contemporaries. This guy gave a really good paper on publishing in London in the middle of the nineteenth century. I'd met him before. He had been very supportive of my work. We talked, and everything came out that was happening with Steve. We ended up spending the night together. He saw how much I had been missing out, how limited my life had become with Steve."

"This guy's name is?" Sandy asked.

"William Keener," Gretchen said. "Bill."

"Did you know Steve was having an affair when this happened?" Sandy asked.

"I hadn't confronted Steve, but I knew it was going on," Gretchen said. "He was vague about where he was. There were calls he got at odd times. I knew. It was amazing to watch him. How could he believe I was so stupid? But he just kept going and going. It is amazing to watch your partner just out-and-out lie to you."

"So now you're both having affairs," Sandy said.

"I would never have had an affair if Steve hadn't been having one," Gretchen snapped. Angry, tired. "I was desperate. I was miserable. Everything was crumbling."

"Gretchen, I'm not making any value judgments here," Sandy said. "But I want to get things straight. Did you talk to Steve about thinking he was having an affair?"

"Yes," Gretchen said. "Right after I got back from that Dickens conference. I told him I knew that he was having an affair. He admitted it. He told me that he'd stopped seeing her a few weeks before."

"Does Steve know about Bill?"

"He probably knows something is going on, I went to the conference, and I came back a different woman," Gretchen said. "But I haven't told him."

"Where is Bill?"

"He teaches at UCLA and he lives in Santa Monica. There's another problem. He's married. And he's also been divorced, which was one reason it was so good to talk to him. He knew exactly what I was going through."

"And he has children?" Sandy asked.

"One from each marriage," Gretchen said.

"So how does he get to talk to you for an hour late at night?" Sandy asked.

"He got up in the middle of the night and went into his study," Gretchen said.

"I have a suggestion," Sandy said.

"I know," Gretchen said. "I have to tell Steve."

"That too," Sandy said. "Although I'll bet he knows. My suggestion is this. You are the one in charge here. You may not realize it, but you are in control. Not Bill; not Steve. You are in control of everything right now. My suggestion is that you do exactly what is good for you. For example, put Bill on your schedule."

"How would that work?" Gretchen asked, sounding confused.

"Don't sit around waiting for Bill's wife to go to sleep so that Bill can slip down to his study and give you a call and keep you up all night," Sandy said. "You tell him when it's convenient for you to talk to him."

"He can't just say to his wife, Excuse me, I need to go call Gretchen."

"Maybe not, but that's his problem, not yours," Sandy said.

"I need to talk to him."

"Believe me, he'll figure it out," Sandy said.

"I don't want to stress him out," Gretchen said.

"Him? You've got two little kids you are taking care of on your own, you have papers to grade, you have courses to teach, you have committees you have to go to, and your marriage has fallen apart. Who is the one who's stressed out?" Sandy said.

"I want to talk to him," Gretchen said, tears coming. "I need him." She really was exhausted, Sandy thought. She was a wreck.

"You've got him," Sandy said. "You've done a great job pulling everything apart, but right now you need to pull yourself together."

"I'm in love with him," Gretchen said, the words pouring out. "I can talk to him. I finally have someone I can talk to. For the first time in years. I want him so much it makes me ache inside."

Gretchen looked at Sandy and held her hands out.

"But he's married and he's been divorced once. This is never going to work out. I wish his wife would die," Gretchen said.

She was sobbing now. Sandy handed her the box of tissues she kept on the side table by her chair.

"I am exhausted," Gretchen said.

"I know," Sandy said. "How could you not be?"

3.

Gandy heard Steve's Mercedes, the AMG C63, chug into the parking lot, sounding just like her mother's C63, and it irritated her. Her mother had driven that car not for the comfort of her clients—for a Mercedes it was a little cramped. She wanted power, the big thunking V-8, with low-slung torque that could drive you back in the seat and smoke the rear wheels, feed you with raging intensity, fasten the seat belts, here we come. That was Mom. Is that what you were wanting to project, Steve?

He didn't come up right away. It was four or five minutes before he opened the door to the waiting room, triggering the light under Sandy's desk. Then there was a knock on her office door, and it opened but not all the way. Steve looked in.

"I'm not sure what the protocol is," Steve said. "Do I wait out here until you come and get me?"

"Yes, because someone could still be in here—a crisis," Sandy said. "But no one is here. Come in."

He looked about the same: downcast, depressed, a cracked translucent china plate, like the ones Sandy's mom had bought late in life, porcelain so thin you could see your hand through it.

"Can I get your opinion on something?" he said.

"Sure," Sandy said.

"So I was coming over here from Presidio Heights. I was going down Bush Street. The next thing I knew I was on the Embarcadero. I had overshot Fillmore. I had no memory of having gotten to the Embarcadero. I had to turn around to head back toward Fillmore. Then I was on Fillmore but with no memory of how I got there. Next thing I knew, I was in your parking lot."

"Are you taking drugs, Steve?" Sandy asked. "Drinking?"

It brought him up in the chair, snapped him into the moment, into right now.

"What!" he said. "No, I'm not taking any drugs. Maybe I should, because I'm not sleeping, but I'm not. I'm not drinking. Is that what you think?"

"I have no idea," Sandy said. "I met you once, four days ago. But I know you work in a stressful environment and—"

He cut her off.

"Yes, but I don't take drugs," he said forcefully.

Sandy saw that she had pushed him down to the bottom of his self-respect.

"So what is going on? How are you driving and not knowing where you are?" Sandy asked.

"I was coming to see you, I had a lot on my mind," Steve said. "I guess my mind handed over the driving to my subconscious while I thought about what I was going to say to you."

If he was being cross-examined in a divorce proceeding, is this what he would say? I was driving the kids to school and I handed the wheel over to my subconscious?

But you got here, Sandy thought. She thought: When you're this loose you might be able to change.

"Driving over, you were thinking about what you were going to say to me?" Sandy asked.

"I was going to tell you how hard Gretchen and I had been working," Steve said. "How that got us into trouble. I work with a bunch of insanely driven egomaniacs. I was working flat-out. And Gretchen was killing herself to get tenure. Is it any wonder we got into trouble?"

"There are many couples running flat-out at max, and they don't get into trouble," Sandy said.

"What's their secret?" Steve asked.

"They're helping each other to run flat-out," Sandy said.

"We were doing such different things," Steve said. "It was tough to understand what we were each going through. I didn't know how to help Gretchen get tenure."

"Helping Gretchen get tenure may not be something you could do," Sandy said. "Understanding what she is going through is something else. Getting tenure is a life-changing event. If you don't make it, it's going to kill you. She must have been scared stiff."

"She wasn't scared stiff," Steve said.

"How do you know that?"

"Gretchen was going to get tenure. She was the best thing that ever happened to the English department at USF," he said.

"How do you know? Did she tell you that?" Sandy said. "Do you think Gretchen thought that?"

"I don't know what Gretchen thought because she would never tell me what she thought. She was usually writing a paper at the kitchen table and I had to tiptoe around her, or she was at a conference," Steve said. "I tried to talk to Gretchen about her work, and it just made her angry."

"Explain that to me?" Sandy said.

"She would tell me I didn't understand," Steve said. "That was her mantra: You wouldn't understand."

Sandy thought: How does this relate to what's happening now?

"So how are things going now, this week?" Sandy asked. "The kids? How are they doing?"

"I pick the kids up at after-school day care two afternoons a week, I do something with them until around seven, when I drop them with Gretchen. Then every other weekend, I have them," Steve said.

Sandy noted that Steve had answered a different question from the one she'd asked him.

"Are you happy having the children on such a limited basis?" Sandy asked.

"No," Steve said slowly. "When we separated, this was what Gretchen wanted. I'm just beginning to understand what I want. I want more time with them. It has to change."

"Could you arrange that with your work?" Sandy asked.

"I have an equity interest in the firm now," Steve said. "I could make some sort of deal."

"So they can't fire you?"

"They could, but it would cost them," Steve said. "And now Gretchen has tenure. I suppose if we'd managed to hold on for another year, we would still be together, instead of getting separated."

"There is a lot going on here, Steve," Sandy said. "I think there's a lot of stuff that has nothing to do with your job or Gretchen's. It has to do with how you two relate to each other. You are terrible at communicating with each other."

"Yes, but we can work on it, I hope," Steve said.

"We can try," Sandy said.

"What are our chances of getting back together?" he

asked suddenly. Sandy felt Steve had wanted to ask about this for a while—she wasn't surprised at the question.

"The chances are not good," Sandy said.

"Are they fifty-fifty?" Steve asked.

"More like one in a thousand," Sandy said.

A look of terror and then anger and then incredible sadness swept over Steve.

"How can you know that?" he said, his voice rising.

"You asked me what I thought, and I tried to give you a straight answer," Sandy said.

"I can't accept this," Steve said. "We have to work it out. There must be something I can do."

His desperation moved Sandy. She felt for him. But Steve would have to make huge changes to get back together with Gretchen. It would be a monumental job. On top of that he would need lots of luck.

"Don't some of the people you see get back together?" Steve asked.

"Steve, most of the people I see have intact marriages. They're here to make them better," Sandy said.

"But you've had clients who have been separated, right?" Steve said desperately.

"Of course," Sandy said. "And I've had people who were divorced but had kids together and wanted a good relationship for the sake of their kids."

"Look, haven't you had clients who were separated and managed to get back together?" Steve said.

"A few," Sandy said.

"How many?"

"Two couples," Sandy said. It was the truth. When you got as far down the line as Steve and Gretchen had, it was really hard to slow down the divorce train so you could hop off.

"Two?" Steve said. He looked at Sandy, dumbfounded. As if he'd been shot.

"How long have you been a marriage counselor?" Steve asked.

"This isn't going anywhere," Sandy said.

"Yes it is," Steve said. "I want to know something important. Are we here to make the divorce as peaceful as we can, or are we here to try to repair the relationship?"

"Those two goals aren't mutually exclusive," Sandy said.

"I thought this was marriage counseling," Steve snapped. "As in there is a marriage that we are trying to save. You would like to save this marriage, right?"

"This isn't about me," Sandy said.

"Well, I want to save this marriage," Steve said forcefully.

"Then save it," Sandy said evenly.

Her challenge hung in the air between them.

"I thought you were going to help me figure out how to do that," Steve said after a moment. "Like there would be some sort of plan. For starters we would agree not to sleep with other people. Then we'd identify our problems and try to take them on, one by one. Some sort of action plan."

"I want to make sure you hear me," Sandy said low and hard. "I want you to really listen."

"I'm really listening," Steve said. "Believe me."

"Okay," Sandy said. "There is no action plan. There is no plan at all. And there are not going to be any agreements like you won't sleep with other people. I'm certainly not going to suggest it, because I think it would be the wrong way to go."

"It would be wrong?" Steve said. He looked confused. As if there were no way out.

"It would be useless to suggest it. If Gretchen wants to sleep with someone, she will," Sandy said. "And why shouldn't she? You guys aren't living together."

Steve looked doomed. The jury had come in with a death sentence.

"I will say this," Sandy said. "I remember now that I know three couples who were separated and got back together. My husband and I lived apart for almost a year. We got back together eventually."

This news seemed to lift Steve's spirits.

"You told me to save the marriage," Steve said.

"Yes," Sandy said.

"But you don't have any ideas about how I should do that? Not one? Even though you and your husband managed to get back together?"

"I didn't say I had no ideas," Sandy said. "I have one idea. I think you need to feel better about yourself. I think that is the place to start. You can't do anything about Gretchen right now, but you can do something about yourself. You need to do whatever will make you feel better. And I have another idea.

"I want you to try an exercise: when Gretchen says something, I want you to imagine that she means the opposite of what she is saying."

"Are you saying that Gretchen says the opposite of what she really thinks?"

"Not literally all the time, but sometimes. But that's not important. I want you to think about what's behind what Gretchen is saying, look for the real meaning. If you imagine that she means the opposite of what she's saying, maybe you will be open to the multiple meanings that are possible."

"So if Gretchen says she hates me, she really means she loves me?"

Sandy had to smile.

"It's possible. Or maybe she hates you and loves you. Consider all the possibilities," Sandy said.

4.

Sandy had been thinking about her mom's big black screaming Mercedes, the AMG C63, all morning, and now that she was in her office, she decided she wasn't ready to reach a decision about it. She called the garage, and Don answered.

"Don," Don said.

"Hey, Don, it's Sandy Hyland," Sandy said. "I've decided I'm not ready to sell the car."

"I offered you a good price," Don said. "Did you check it out on Edmunds?"

"It's not about the price," Sandy said. "I'm not ready to sell the Mercedes."

"You drive a Prius," Don said. "What would you want a C63 for?"

Like she had to explain her reasons? She needed some justification for not wanting to sell her mother's car? Would her mother have given Don an explanation?

She hung up on Don. Then she put her desk phone on standby. The only way to reach her now was on her cell and the only one who had her cell number was her answering service, and if it was a real emergency, her cell would vibrate, not ring.

She looked at her watch. She had five minutes. She shut her eyes and breathed deeply. The deep thunk-thunk of Steve's car, the twin to her mother's car, woke her out of it. She gave them a little time to get up the stairs, to settle down in the waiting room. Then she opened the door: they were sitting across from each other, Steve staring into space and Gretchen with a pen in her hand, reading a paper and making comments on it.

"Hey there," Sandy said. "Come on in."

And they did.

"How are you guys doing?" Sandy asked, looking at them, thinking Steve looked somewhat better.

"I have something that I want to discuss," Gretchen said.

"Okay," Sandy said, knowing what was coming.

"I'm in a relationship with someone," Gretchen said briskly. She looked at Sandy, then Steve. "It doesn't feel as if it's your business. But Sandy says we have to be honest with each other or there is no reason to be here at all."

"I knew you were having an affair," Steve said.

"How did you know that?" Sandy asked.

"I've been inside Gretchen's computer," Steve said quietly.

"How did you do that?" Gretchen said angrily.

"We used to live together, I had your passwords, I accessed your computer remotely," Steve said.

"My e-mail?" Gretchen asked.

"Yes," Steve said.

"Was my e-mail informative?" Gretchen spit it out.

"Afterward, I was sorry I did it," Steve said. "I did it once. I was crazy, I couldn't stand what was happening to us. It won't happen again."

"It certainly won't," Gretchen said forcefully. "I'm changing all my passwords. I'm taking my laptop to the university IT department and having them go through it to see if you've put any bugs in it, and then having them install the best privacy software they have."

"I told you I'm not going to go into your computer again," Steve said. "But do whatever you want."

"As if you could stop me," Gretchen said. "What else have you done?"

Sandy guessed what Steve had done. Of course, Steve

would do a better job than most injured husbands. He was a creative, hard-driving guy, a force to be reckoned with.

"I'm sorry about this, but I couldn't help myself. At the time, I was out-of-my-mind jealous and scared," Steve said. "I commissioned a full report on Bill."

"What does that mean?" Gretchen said.

"The kind of report we get on the principals, when we're buying a business," Steve said. "Have they ever been arrested? Did they pay their taxes?"

"Are they having an affair on the side?" Gretchen asked.

"It's come up in the reports," Steve said.

"When you got this report, did I come up?" Gretchen asked.

"No," Steve said. "You didn't come up."

"I really, really am so sick of you," Gretchen said. "How can you be so controlling?"

How could he be so miserable, Sandy thought.

"So what did you think?" Sandy asked Steve, curious.

"About what?" Steve said.

"What did you think after you read your report on Bill?"

"Does it really matter?" Gretchen said. "What matters is that he did it in the first place."

"I think it matters," Sandy said. "I want to know what Steve thought about the report. Don't you?"

"I'm having a hard time just getting through the fact he investigated Bill," Gretchen said. "It's crazy."

"It was a dumb thing to do. I can see that," Steve said.

"Dumb? To me it seems like a natural reaction." Sandy looked at Gretchen, then back at Steve. "Am I the only one who is interested in the report?" she said. "Steve, tell me what you thought after you'd read it."

He paused. He was unsure about explaining what he thought. He was used to being able to hide difficult stuff from Gretchen. Sandy wanted to grab Steve by the lapels and shake him.

"It sounds like Bill is a very good teacher," Steve said, picking his words carefully, cautiously. "Very involved with his students. He's won several teaching awards. His students seem to like him a lot."

Sandy thought about the way Gretchen and Steve were entwined together, trapped together, how both of them tried to avoid talking about the hard stuff. Would they rather get divorced than talk about the difficult issues between them? Maybe.

"Steve, I don't believe you came away from reading this report thinking what a good teacher Bill was," Sandy said.

"He is a good teacher," Gretchen said. "Bill is a great teacher."

"I came away thinking I was in trouble, if you want to know the truth," Steve said.

You are in trouble, Sandy thought.

"I could see he could be a very persuasive man, I could see that he might be exactly what Gretchen wanted. A sensitive, articulate guy who she could share her work with, both of them teaching college English."

"He is a sensitive, articulate man," Gretchen said. "He is also honest, and caring."

"I wasn't so sure about the honest and caring part," Steve said. "He left his first wife and a young child for a student."

"She was a graduate student," Gretchen said, stone-cold.

"He was supervising her thesis, he was her mentor," Steve said.

"This stuff is in the report? Fuck," Gretchen said, warming.

"He got divorced. They went to court. There is a public record," Steve said. "His first wife was really mad when she found out about the graduate student."

"You are hardly one to talk about cheating on your wife," Gretchen said.

"No, I'm not," Steve said quietly. "I am very, very sorry for what I did, and I wish I could undo it. I really don't want to lose you."

"You lost me a long time ago," Gretchen snapped. "Bill helped me to leave you, he gave me strength, he was a gift. But he didn't have anything to do with why I left you. You caused that to happen all on your own."

Gretchen sat back, she folded her arms across her chest. Then she looked at Sandy.

"What am I going to do?" Gretchen said. "Is there any way to stop him?"

Stop him from being human? Sandy wondered.

"Why do you want to stop him?" Sandy said. "Everything that Steve did is predictable. If you thought about it, you knew he would do it. What I'm interested in is why you didn't realize he would do it. Why are you surprised? You shouldn't be. We should deal with that and we will. But let me ask: Was it so terrible?"

"He invaded my privacy," Gretchen said, sitting up ramrod-straight in her chair. "It is a personal violation."

"Why is it a personal violation?" Sandy said.

"He invaded my privacy," Gretchen repeated stubbornly. "Of course that's personal."

"Really? I mean, so what?" Sandy said. "You're married. You are supposed to talk to each other. Were you talking to Steve?"

"I want autonomy," Gretchen said. "Steve never gave it to me."

"I get that," Sandy said. "But let's put that aside for a moment, because it is another big issue. We need to feel our way toward it. Let's deal with the issue at hand. I'm sure Steve made himself feel a lot worse than you're feeling now. He went on your computer and discovered how much you love some other guy, and then he commissioned a report that told him that Bill was a charismatic guy and a real threat."

Sandy turned and looked at Steve.

"How much did the report cost?" Sandy asked.

"Fifteen hundred dollars," Steve said.

"It must have hurt," Sandy said.

"You can't imagine," Steve said.

"Oh, yes I can," Sandy said. "Have you learned anything?"

"I'm feeling sort of dead right now," Steve said, sounding down, defeated, depressed. "Like I've been paralyzed and can't move. It's hard to explain. I feel like I'm just going to be tossed around by a huge storm and I can't control anything, the storm is just going to throw me wherever. Just wherever."

"That's a good statement of what you've learned," Sandy said. "I think that is an honest description of how you feel right now. I also think it is a good thing that you feel you can't control anything."

Steve looked at Sandy as if she were completely crazy. It was not the first time he had looked at Sandy that way. And Sandy was pretty sure it was not going to be the last.

"I'm lost," Gretchen said. She sat up in her chair, crossed her arms, then looked back at Sandy. "What has he learned?"

"That he can't control anything," Sandy said. "That he can't control you. That he's got to let go. He has to let go of you. He has no choice. The storm is going to take him wherever it wants. You are the storm. He's not going to fight you. He can't."

Gretchen took that in. After a moment, she nodded.

"Does that mean he doesn't fuck with my computer? With my privacy? With Bill? With my life?" Gretchen said to Sandy.

Gretchen doesn't get it, Sandy thought. She was surprised. Sandy looked at Steve.

"Yes," Steve said. "I'm not going to invade your privacy again."

Sandy was still staring at Steve.

"Of course you will invade her privacy. You'll do it again, and again," Sandy said. "And it will often be a good thing. This is a really hard lesson to learn. Where the boundaries are. When to cross over them. If you learn it, it will take you months or years. Here is something simple to learn right now: You both need to tell each other everything, but you can't demand that. You have to make the other *want* to tell you everything. You can't make them. That never works."

"Why not?" Steve said. "Why couldn't we just agree to tell each other everything?"

"You already tried that," Sandy said. "See how well it worked?"

She meant, you agreed to that when you got married, and Sandy could see that both of them understood what she meant.

Could they go further? she wondered. She looked at Steve.

"Let me ask you a question. If I had a magic button and pressed it, Bill would just evaporate. It would be as if he had never existed. Now suppose I handed that button to you, would you press it?"

Steve looked at Sandy. He looked over at Gretchen, then back at Sandy. A thought flicked across his face, a ripple over the dark sea.

"No, I wouldn't press it," Steve said.

5.

"*You guys got together* in college, right?" Sandy said.

"Yes," Gretchen said. "I was a freshman, but I had sophomore standing, so I could take pretty much any course I wanted. Steve was a junior. We met in class."

"What class?" Sandy asked.

"Elizabethan poetry," Gretchen said finally.

"A seminar?" Sandy asked.

"A seminar," Gretchen said. "I'm not sure, but I think there were perhaps twelve students in the class."

"And somehow Steve came to your attention," Sandy said. "Why?"

Gretchen looked at the ceiling for a moment, and then back at Sandy.

"There were only twelve students in the class, you pretty much notice everyone," she said evenly.

"Maybe I phrased it wrong," Sandy said. "You first met Steve in an Elizabethan poetry seminar. From there it led to a love affair. Why?"

"Do we need to talk about this?" Gretchen said.

"Humor me," Sandy said.

"You want to explain it?" Gretchen said to Steve. He shook his head.

"So the professor was trying to make some broad points about how Elizabethan poetry was different from, say, modern poetry. Anyway, there were some pretty affected guys in the class, sort of mega-intellectual guys. With scarves. You know. And then there was Steve, who looked like he'd just blown in from L.A. or something."

A little change took place. Sandy saw not a smile, not anything you could define precisely, but Gretchen was looking sort of into the middle distance. She was going back to that moment.

"Anyway, there was a huge amount of stupid convoluted stuff being bantered around. You know, whenever someone talks about semantics I get nervous. And that was the general direction we were going in. Semiotics and hermeneutics.

"But we all had the book right in front of us, and on the cover was a picture of Queen Elizabeth. All dressed up with this incredible ruff thing around her neck, this dress with billowing sleeves that was covered with tiny pearls in intricate designs. And Steve said that if we wanted to understand the difference between Elizabethan poetry and modern poetry, maybe we ought to think about the difference between Elizabethan dress and modern dress. And he held up the book. I noticed him when he suggested that. The professor noticed too."

Gretchen crossed her arms and sat back.

"That's a nice story," Sandy said. "I want to try something. Gretchen, I want you to look at Steve and tell me what you see now."

But Gretchen didn't look at Steve. She said: "I'm so fed up with Steve, I'm not sure I can see him objectively."

"So don't be objective. Just look at Steve," Sandy said. "Describe him the way you would any object. What do you see?"

Gretchen looked at Steve, in a cursory way, as if he weren't of much interest. She said nothing.

She's beginning to tick me off, Sandy realized. She stared at Gretchen and said nothing.

"You want me to just describe him?" Gretchen asked after a few more seconds.

"Yes," Sandy said flatly, thinking, Isn't that what I asked?

"Okay," Gretchen said. She perked up. "I see a guy in his mid-thirties, he's got brown hair, brown eyes. He wears yellow glasses. He has on a blue button-down shirt, cords, driving shoes. How's that?"

That was pretty good, Sandy thought, these two are good little wonks, you give them an assignment, they can't help themselves, they want to do a good job.

"I think you could go a little further," Sandy pushed.

"You're pushing me, but that's okay," Gretchen said, Sandy noticing their minds were now in sync.

Gretchen looked hard at Steve.

"Everything about him is kind of perfect," Gretchen said. "He has a silver belt buckle, and it's polished. His shirt is ironed nicely. He has a great haircut and it's pretty recent. Those yellow glasses? I happen to know they're Italian. Very stylish. So I guess I think he's looking casual, but he's put in a lot of effort to do it."

"A little further?" Sandy said.

"You're not making this easy," Gretchen said. Gretchen looked hard at Steve, taking him in for a good minute. Sandy noticed that Steve reacted to Gretchen's stare, looking away toward the window.

Gretchen said, "I think Steve has a sort of boyish look."

"How do you mean boyish?" Sandy asked.

"I may be reading too much into this," Gretchen said.

"It's like he's really trying hard. He wants to look all grown-up, and he's trying so hard. You feel as if you don't want to pop his balloon. You want to tell him, Nice job, you look good."

"That was a good effort," Sandy said, and then looked at Steve.

"Steve, are you trying hard to look good?" Sandy said.

"Yes," Steve said. "I am. It's sort of a big deal to come here. It *is* a big deal to come here. So yes, I'm trying to look good, I think about what I'm wearing when I come here."

Steve threw his arms out, an expression that said something like What do you expect?

"I mean, I'm nervous," he said.

"What are you nervous about?" Sandy asked.

"For one thing, my marriage is on the line," Steve said. "That's a pretty big thing. I guess I want to do all I can to try to get my marriage back on track."

He sighed. He looked uncomfortable.

"When we first separated, I felt as if I was in a dense fog. I was disoriented. It was hard to make even small decisions. I remember I went to a cash machine. I put in my card. And then I couldn't remember my PIN. I couldn't remember four numbers that I had been using it seemed like all my life. After a while, I canceled the transaction, took my card, and went and sat in my car.

"I sat there for like half an hour and then, by some miracle, my PIN floated up to me as if it were coming to the surface of a lake. And I went and got two hundred dollars out.

"I don't mean to go on and on," Steve said.

Sandy saw that Gretchen was staring at Steve, giving him her complete attention.

"Go on and on," Sandy said. "Please."

"So, anyway, it was like I needed to teach myself how to do things. The first thing I did was I gave my car an inspection. I checked the oil, I checked the tires, the water, everything. I wanted to make sure that I had the basics covered. Then I sat down at my desk and checked all my accounts and all the bills. I hadn't paid any attention to that stuff for weeks.

"It was like I was creating myself from the ground up. So, that's why my shirt is pressed, and my hair is cut. I feel as if I need to make sure I tackle the little things. All the things that most people take for granted, I have to make sure I'm doing them. I'm still having trouble."

"Gretchen, what Steve said, does it make you see him any differently?" Sandy asked.

"I never thought I could knock Steve back on his heels," Gretchen said. "I'm still surprised. I didn't realize he was so vulnerable. So, I want to make a connection. I said he seemed boyish, young. What I was seeing was that he was vulnerable. I used to be scared of Steve."

"I'm sorry I made you scared," Steve said.

"Don't worry about it," Gretchen said. "You don't make me scared anymore. In fact, you don't make me feel anything anymore."

"Okay," Sandy said. "Now it's your turn, Steve. Can you describe Gretchen?"

"One thing first," Steve said. "Right after we first split up, I said it was like I was in a deep fog? The one thing I could see clearly was Gretchen. It was as if I hadn't been looking, but now I saw her really clearly."

Steve looked at Gretchen.

"So I see a really beautiful woman. I see blond hair, blue eyes, I see that she's not wearing a wedding ring. I see that she has little gold circle earrings, a gold watch. No other jewelry. She's wearing stretchy jeans, a white shirt, black shoes. Flats, no heels. I see the brown leather purse on the floor, which I know comes from Bottega Veneta because I bought it for her."

He looked away from Gretchen.

"Can you see more?" Sandy said.

"This is making me feel sad," Steve said. "I can't believe I ever hurt you."

"Well, you did," Gretchen said. "But it's not going to happen again."

"What do you see?" Sandy said.

"Gretchen, you look as if you're only partly here," Steve said slowly. "I don't think you're engaged with me. A part of you is far away."

"You're right," Gretchen said. "I can't help it. I'm trying to be engaged with you. I'm coming to these sessions. But it's hard to be with you, Steve."

Gretchen looked at Sandy.

"When I was describing Steve, I felt detached, almost clinical," Gretchen said.

"I know," Sandy said.

"I'm holding him at a distance," Gretchen said.

"That's okay," Sandy said. "You need to."

"If I can't empathize with Steve, then this isn't ever going to work, is it?" Gretchen said. She pushed back in her chair. She seemed fragile to Sandy. Now she looked at Steve again.

"I just can't believe you put everything we had at risk. I mean, how could you be such an idiot?" Gretchen said to him.

"I can explain how I could be such a complete idiot," Steve said.

"I already know," Gretchen said. "You were miserable. Our life made you miserable."

"I had made myself miserable," Steve said.

"So you made us both miserable," Gretchen said. "That was *smart*."

That was *smart*. She hit the word hard.

Steve was reaching out to Gretchen, and she beat him back with sarcasm and contempt. Steve kept coming. He dusted himself off, and made sure his shirt was pressed and his buckle was polished, and he went at it again.

Look at him, Gretchen, Sandy thought. Really look at him. Look how he comes back again and again to you.

6.

The boom-boom of Steve's big car ...

They came in one right after the other. Gretchen first, then Steve.

Gretchen was skittish, energetic. She sort of pranced into the office. Steve was glowering, looking down.

They sat in their usual places. Sandy looked them over, trying to get out in front of them. There was tension. They were wired, nervous. Sandy felt a bit like a cowgirl, working a cattle herd that was on the edge of a stampede, the kind of herd that takes off wildly heading for a cliff, and the cowboys try to turn the herd back toward safer ground. *Turn them, head them off . . .*

"So what's going on?" Sandy said. "I sense something is."

"As a matter of fact there is something going on," Gretchen said. "I'm going to a conference at NYU in two weeks. I'm going to be gone five days. Thursday, Friday, and then over the weekend, and I return on Monday. So the idea is that Steve would take the kids while I'm away. I was thinking that it would probably work best if he had them at his parents' house, but Steve doesn't seem to like that idea. So we need your help to resolve the issues."

"The conference doesn't go over the weekend," Steve said evenly. "It runs Thursday and Friday. Gretchen is staying over in New York City."

"Apparently Steve did a little research," Gretchen said. "That's predictable. Just like you said, Sandy."

It was predictable and human and Gretchen didn't seem angry about Steve's research. Good for you, Gretchen. So what is this about?

"Your friend Bill is going to the conference, and you two are staying over the weekend?" Sandy said.

"I don't know that it's anyone's business, but yes, something like that," Gretchen said. "But not exactly. We're not staying in New York City over the weekend. We're going to an inn up the Hudson River."

Sandy noticed Steve flinch when Gretchen said *inn*.

"Can I ask a personal question?" Steve said.

Gretchen immediately saw where this was going. Sandy saw her sit up in her chair.

"I don't know, Steve," Gretchen said.

You only know if you know the question.

"What is the question?" Sandy said.

"I would like to know if Bill has told his wife about his affair with Gretchen," Steve said.

Gretchen stood up.

"That is despicable," she said. "I can't believe you. That's it. This is over."

"Sit down," Sandy said. She said it as if she were in complete command. Her office, her chair, her rules. She had no idea if Gretchen would obey her, but in fact she sat.

"Why is that such an outlandish question?" Sandy asked.

"It's . . ." Gretchen struggled for a second. "It's a way for Steve to say that Bill is a terrible person. He hasn't told his wife. He has been divorced. He doesn't see the kid from his first marriage. Everything Steve asks about Bill is designed to make him look bad."

"I have never asked you about Bill's kids from any of his marriages," Steve said.

Oh, Steve, give it up, Sandy thought. Give up all the little issues.

"If you give me this literal shit of yours, I'm going to hit you," Gretchen said. She was beginning to rise out of her chair again. Sandy spread her arms wide in front of her, like a conductor leading toward a quiet part of the symphony.

"What does it matter if Bill has told his wife about the affair with Gretchen?" Sandy asked, looking at Steve.

"Okay," Steve said. "Look. I just looked up the conference and saw that it only went two days. It didn't take any special talent. I googled the conference. His wife can do the same. Isn't she going to wonder why her husband is staying two extra days?"

"Why would you care if she does wonder?" Sandy said.

Steve shut down, drew into himself and looked toward the window. No you don't, Steve, Sandy thought.

"You had something on your mind," Sandy said. "What was it?"

"I thought she might go nuts," Steve said quietly.

"So she goes nuts," Sandy said. "Isn't that Bill's problem?"

"Unless she goes violent," Steve said. "Unless she wants revenge."

"Oh for God's sake," Gretchen said. "You're worried Bill's wife is going to kill me?"

"No," Steve said. He paused, thinking over what he was going to say. Knowing where this was going. Scared. Go on, Sandy thought, wanting to push him. "I was worried she might kill our kids."

"Fuck," Gretchen said. "What is wrong with you?"

It was such an outlandish statement. Weren't they all

solid middle-class people? Of course they wouldn't do something like that. But they might, Sandy thought.

"What made you think that?" Sandy asked Steve.

"I don't know," Steve said.

"I think you do," Sandy said. Her voice was like the voice of your mother on a dark night when you can't sleep. Sandy could do that trick when she had to.

"Okay," Steve said. "I've had a fantasy about killing Bill."

"But you wouldn't do that, would you?" Sandy said.

Steve had been looking down, now he looked up at Sandy and then over at Gretchen.

"No, I *wouldn't*," he said. "I wouldn't press the button you talked about and I wouldn't kill him. There would always be another guy."

Usually, Sandy didn't pay much attention to the world beyond her small office. The illicit meeting in New York. Where Gretchen was going for the weekend. What Bill's wife knew. Everything that happened outside the office? She didn't care.

To Sandy, the important story was what happened inside her office.

It was what she had to focus on, it was the *story*, it was what was really happening. Of course, all the time, it was tempting to get caught up in the outside story. The affairs, the sex, the betrayals! The soap opera. But the real work was here, inside her office.

"I don't mind taking the kids," Steve said, sliding off the issue of someone killing the kids. Sandy let him slide.

"Can I say something?" Gretchen said, sliding off that issue too. "Steve says he *doesn't mind* taking the kids. Like it's something he chooses to do. I have a problem with that. He is supposed to want to take care of his kids. It's not an optional choice, though that's how he's treating it."

"I want to take care of the kids," Steve said. "Okay?"

"Then do it, and don't complain about it," Gretchen ordered.

"Can we just back up for a moment," Sandy said. "Gretchen, you said it was predictable that Steve would research this conference. If you knew he would do it, why didn't you just tell him the whole story?"

"It's none of his business," Gretchen said. She said it sincerely, Sandy felt, she honestly didn't see why she should confide in Steve about her love life. And it was a valid point, sort of.

"But here we are talking about it, both of you angry," Sandy said. "What would have happened if you'd just said, Look, I'm going to New York for a conference, and then I'm going to stick around and spend some time with my friend, so can you take the kids for four days?"

"Am I supposed to tell Steve about my love life?" Gretchen said.

It would help, Sandy thought.

"I'm not sure saying what you're doing while he's got the

kids is telling him your love life," Sandy said. "But anyway, if you had told Steve what was going on, then he wouldn't be stalking you."

"I'm not stalking her," Steve said.

"Whatever you want to call it," Gretchen said. "What do you call it, Steve?"

He didn't answer. So we'll call it stalking, Sandy thought.

"I'd like to go back to my question," Sandy said. "Steve, how would you have felt if Gretchen had told you she was going to see her friend?"

"I would have been angry," Steve said. Then he hesitated, thinking. "Okay, I would have been hurt. But at least I would have felt like we trusted each other a little bit."

"Look, are you telling me that I'm supposed to tell Steve every time I see someone?" Gretchen said. "I want a life of my own. We are not living together anymore."

"You have the kids during the week, right? And if I remember correctly, this weekend you're going away is a weekend that you would have ordinarily had the kids, right?" Sandy said. "Have you ever asked Steve to take the kids for you? Is this the first time?"

"This is the first time," Gretchen said.

"So this is sort of a big deal, isn't it," Sandy said.

"A big deal because Steve has the kids for four days?" Gretchen snapped. "Yes, that is a big, big deal, I admit that. It's the first time he's had the kids alone for four days in his life. But I don't want to explain my life to him. That's another issue."

"I think all this stuff is connected," Sandy said.

Why are you so defended, Gretchen? Sandy wondered. Why does this touch a nerve? She had a pretty good idea what was going on. It would have been great if Steve did too. It would have made him feel better.

Sandy thought: Gretchen has doubts about the weekend she plans to spend with Bill. She feels vulnerable, unsure about it. A part of her doesn't want to go away for the weekend. But this is stuff she's not going to discuss with you, Steve, not yet anyway. Steve, when you asked if Bill had told his wife about Gretchen, you hit Gretchen's vulnerability. Yes, she's worried that Bill is just playing her . . .

They all sat for a few moments, letting everything subside.

"You said you wanted Steve to take the kids to his parents' for the four days?" Sandy said finally. "Why was that, Gretchen, why his parents?"

"To give Steve some backup," Gretchen said. "His parents have a big house, and they like the kids. Steve is in a one-bedroom apartment. At his place, it's sort of like camping out."

"Why do you have a one-bedroom apartment?" Sandy asked, looking at Steve.

"It's all crazy," Steve said. "Gretchen was moving to the city. We were selling our house. I had moved to my parents'.

I came upon this apartment that was near Gretchen's new apartment. I think there was a sign up or something. I just rented it. I wasn't thinking. I was in a fog. I looked at it for maybe five minutes and I told the moving guys to take my stuff directly from our old house to this apartment. They were in the process of moving Gretchen's stuff into her new apartment. You know what the movers said?"

Amazingly, Steve smiled for a moment.

"They said, Man, why are you giving her all the good stuff? You're giving her the piano, the sofas, the chairs. I said she had a bigger apartment, she could fit them in. They said, Why does she have a bigger apartment?

"But it wasn't as if I was really giving Gretchen anything. It was like I was on the *Titanic* and the ship was going down, and all the stuff on the ship was floating away."

The mood had changed for Steve. He wasn't as angry anymore. He had accepted it all: Gretchen's weekend in New York, her new friend, their separation. For this small moment, he had some perspective.

"From a practical point of view, it might have been better if I'd told Steve about my plans for the weekend," Gretchen said. "If he was going to find out about it anyway."

"From a practical point of view, you're going to want to know how the kids are doing while you're away, aren't you?" Sandy said.

That caught Gretchen up. Sandy thought that Gretchen might not have thought about the issue at all.

"Yes, I will," Gretchen said.

"How are you planning on doing that?"

"I guess I'll text Steve," Gretchen said. "To see how things are going. Or he'll text me."

"And if there is a big problem, then what?" Sandy said.

"Then I guess he calls me," Gretchen said.

And the same thing happens for your friend's kids and his wife, doesn't it, Sandy thought. Only, he's lying to his wife. You aren't, Gretchen. You are ahead of the game.

"Yes, I should have told Steve what was happening on that weekend," Gretchen said. "I see it."

She looked over at Steve.

"Is there anything you want to know about the weekend?" Gretchen asked him.

"I know enough," Steve said.

7.

They weren't done with the New York trip. The next session:

"I want to revisit what happens next weekend, the weekend you go away, where I said I would take the kids to my parents' house," Steve said.

Gretchen shot Steve a pained look.

"We had a deal on what was happening that weekend," she said.

"It wasn't like anyone took a blood oath," Sandy said. She hated deals. "Why don't we hear what Steve has to say?"

Deals freeze things, Sandy thought. Who would want to freeze this marriage where it was? Why were they here?

"I'm not really in the mood to spend the weekend with my parents," Steve said. "I'm thinking of taking the kids up to Mendocino and visiting with the Snyders."

"You're kidding me," Gretchen said. "Come on. Fuck you, Steve."

"Who are the Snyders?" Sandy asked.

"Very old friends," Steve said. "I went to grammar school with Tina Snyder."

"They are hippies," Gretchen said.

"Tina Snyder went to Bryn Mawr, for Christ's sake," Steve said.

"She's an airhead trust-fund baby," Gretchen said.

"They have an organic farm," Steve said. "Tina's husband, Spencer, did graduate work in agriculture at Davis."

Bryn Mawr? Tina Snyder? Organic farm? Spencer? Who are these people? Get ahold of yourself, Sandy, she told herself.

"This just isn't acceptable to me," Gretchen said. "And it really ticks me off to have to deal with it at the last minute."

"I don't want to upset you," Steve said. "But now that I'm face-to-face with it, the thought of spending the whole weekend with my parents is just not a lot of fun. Would you like to spend the weekend with your parents?"

"I would, I don't get to see my parents all that often," Gretchen said. "Can't you just go with the plan for this weekend and then the next weekend you can visit the Snyders on your own?"

"I don't get what bothers you so much about this," Sandy said to Gretchen.

"We went over this last time," Gretchen said. "I would like the kids in a safe environment while I'm away. I don't trust Steve to take care of them. And the kids will run wild at that farm."

"Why can't you trust Steve?" Sandy asked.

"He wasn't trustworthy before. I doubt he's suddenly changed," Gretchen said. "I feel fine with Steve saying to his mother, Could you watch the kids for a while, I'm tired. I do trust his mother. But I don't feel good about Steve saying that to Tina Snyder, who is a moron."

"Why would Steve turn over the kids to a moron?" Sandy said. A moron who went to Bryn Mawr?

"Steve has a very limited attention span with the kids," Gretchen said. "Tina Snyder has a limited attention span with everything."

"It is true that when I was working flat-out there were times when I was so dead tired that I didn't want to be with the kids, and there were times when I just was stupid," Steve said. "But things have changed. I'm enjoying being with the kids. They're great." He looked at Gretchen. "You do know that I love them?"

"Congratulations on realizing that you love your kids," Gretchen said. "But you should have been spending time with them all along."

"I know that," Steve said.

Sandy watched as Gretchen tightened up.

"Okay, I won't go away for the weekend. I'll fly back Friday night," Gretchen said.

"Wait a minute, Gretchen," Sandy said. "That isn't a resolution. You don't get to grab the ball and go home. It doesn't sound to me that this farm in Mendocino is very dangerous."

"It isn't," Steve said. "It's bunny rabbits and goats. It's organic vegetables."

"It's chaotic," Gretchen said angrily.

"So what?" Steve said. "So what!" He sounded exasperated. "I mean, what's so new with that? When we first separated, I felt like I'd been hit in the head with a sledgehammer. I was dazed. I was in a fog. That was chaotic! I almost had a car accident with the kids. Now I'm gradually coming out of that chaos. I'm beginning to see that I have some options. I can make plans."

"Have you fried your brain, Steve?" Gretchen said.

"Where does that come from?" Sandy asked.

"We have been to that farm once in ten years. Steve hated the place. Didn't you? Tell Sandy," Gretchen said.

"I was an idiot," Steve said with emotion. "I was intolerant. I was judgmental. I regret so many things. Can't I change?"

I hope you can, Sandy thought.

Steve shook his head and looked at Gretchen, wanting forgiveness and absolution.

Fat chance, Sandy thought.

"I'm really looking forward to going back up and seeing the Snyders' farm with fresh eyes," Steve said with feeling.

My God. Sandy saw that Gretchen had tears at the corners of her eyes.

"What did you think about the Snyders' farm?" Sandy asked Gretchen.

"I just told you," Gretchen said.

"No, you didn't," Sandy said. "You told me what Steve thought about it."

"Can't you see that Steve is just doing this to hurt me for going to New York?" Gretchen said.

"Again, you're telling me about Steve's thoughts and motives," Sandy said. "I'm asking about yours."

"Are you fucking taking his side?" Gretchen growled. Low. "I mean, we had a deal here. He was taking the kids to his parents'."

"He wants to take the kids to an organic farm," Sandy said. "That's what this is about. Why do you object to it? What do *you* think about the Snyders' farm?"

"Nothing," Gretchen said. "Actually I'm really angry about this whole thing. Very, very angry."

"I see that, I hear you," Sandy said. "But I don't understand it."

"Neither do I," Steve said.

There was a pause. Gretchen was looking into the middle ground.

She tried to say something, and then she needed more time to get ready. Then finally, she was.

"I loved the Snyders' farm," Gretchen said softly. "I wanted it, all of it. Every perfect carrot. Every fucking little bunny. Every happy moronic goat. I wanted them all."

She flicked her sad eyes over at Steve.

"I wanted to go back there, but you never would," Gretchen said quietly.

Everything stopped for a moment while Steve and Gretchen looked at each other, Gretchen expressing her hurt and Steve beginning to understand how badly he had hurt her.

"I'm so sorry," he said.

8.

Gandy pulled into the small parking lot beside her building. She turned off the engine and just sat there. It was a luxurious feeling, just sitting in her parked car. She didn't have to call her mother's several doctors, or lawyers, or the assisted-care facility. She didn't have to visit any of them either. It had been a hectic three weeks, getting Heidi into the Oaks, with her mother kicking and screaming the whole time. Now that part was over.

In her condo, three weeks ago, Heidi had forgotten to turn the water off in her bathtub and had the safety drain blocked off because she liked the bath full to the top of the tub—and so for half an hour, the water just poured down onto the bathroom floor and then poured down into the apartment below. Well, it was just water, but Sandy could see that the next time it was going to be the gas stove, and maybe her mother would blow the front off the building.

The way it was supposed to go, your mother recognized that there was a problem and together with her daughter they solved it. Not with Heidi. Sandy had to get the doctors and the lawyer on her side, and together they had to threaten her mother, and even then Heidi hired a driver to take her to the weekend house in Inverness, locking the doors and camping out there. It was one thing after another, bang, bang, Sandy putting out fire after fire.

But now it was done, and her mother was in the Oaks, which had impeccable security. Let Heidi try a run to Inverness now. There were hidden cameras in the light fixtures, the only way out was through the lobby, and there were guards on every door. Sure, it looked like a fancy hotel, but it was really a maximum-security facility for difficult troublemakers, rich old ones.

Yes, at some point Sandy would have to deal with selling her mother's C63 Mercedes, and the apartment. But she could take her time, do these jobs in an orderly way.

Sandy got out of her Prius, locked the doors, and saw the

sleeping bag at the edge of the parking lot. Her homeless person. No doubt Heidi would have turned the hose on him, or perhaps even run him over. Or at minimum called the police.

What happened to his shopping cart? She didn't see one. She thought about how her mother was at the Oaks, one hundred fifty thousand dollars a year, and her guy was in a sleeping bag. You got off so easy, Mom. But her mom hadn't gotten off easy, she'd fought life to a standstill. The ref had told life and her mother to go to their corners. They sat there, looking at each other, waiting for the next round, for the bell to ring.

Sandy took twenty dollars out of her wallet and walked carefully to the sleeping bag. Silently, she bent down and slipped the bill under the edge of the bag.

Sandy went up the stairs, past the plaque her mother had put on the side of the building before she gave it to Sandy. She stopped and looked at the plaque. A GIFT FROM HEIDI HYLAND TO HER LOVING DAUGHTER SANDY, WHO THANKS HER FOR HER GENEROSITY. The inscription written by her mother, who had commissioned the plaque. Well, it was a nice building. Thanks, Mom.

Sandy climbed the stairs, unlocked the door to her office suite, and went through the waiting room into her office. She sat down at the desk.

No calls, no appointments, just Steve and Gretchen in fifteen minutes and three other clients later in the day, which stretched out before her like a placid lake.

She looked around her office, coming to rest on the green chair. Neither Steve nor Gretchen had asked her about it. What it was doing there, seemingly so out of touch with the rest of the office.

Sandy looked at her watch, she still had five minutes. In her peripheral vision, she saw movement. She looked back at the green chair. Did you come in, she wondered, are you there?

9.

"*Have you talked* to each other since Gretchen got back from New York?" Sandy asked.

"Not really," Steve said.

"I was exhausted," Gretchen said. "Then we had to deal with transferring the kids from Steve to me."

Gretchen looked at Steve.

"If there is anything you want to know about the trip, ask me," she said.

"Did you have a good time?" Steve asked.

"Some of it was good and some of it was not so good," Gretchen said. "How about you at the Snyders' farm?"

"Tina asked me what I would do if you didn't come back from New York and went to live with Bill. I thought that was a pretty good question. And I realized that what I would do is get a house and move into it with the kids, and raise them by myself," Steve said.

Gretchen frowned. "That would never happen, Steve. If something happened to me, you would find someone else in a day or two and she would raise the kids," Gretchen said.

"I don't think so," Steve said. "But the point is that Tina was really challenging me, because in a sense you *have* gone away. That got me thinking. I mean, why aren't I raising the kids? Why do I only have them for a weekend every two weeks?"

"And you have them after school two days a week," Gretchen said.

"Right," Steve said. "Okay. Let me tell you something else about the Snyders' farm that hit me. Everywhere you look there are projects going on. Each one of the kids has a little garden. And they're growing what they want, not what their parents tell them to grow. And Otis, the oldest one, is raising a pig that he wants to take to 4-H shows. The little girl, Dolly, is raising frogs."

Sandy watched the darkness slowly sweeping in over Gretchen's face. Every fucking bunny, Gretchen?

"It's so amazing how many animals they have. Geese, rabbits, chickens, frogs. The kids are having such rich lives . . ." Steve said.

Gretchen cut in: "Steve, they live in Mendocino. They are isolated. Is that what you want for our kids? Are you kidding? Move to a farm?"

Our kids? Sandy thought. Gretchen was trying to turn the conversation in a safer direction.

"Of course not, but what hit me was that I don't have any projects with our kids. Nothing. We aren't building anything, we aren't raising anything. So I want to start doing that."

"So do projects if you want to," Gretchen said. "No one's stopping you."

Oh, Gretchen, Sandy thought. Face up to the runaway train speeding down the track to where you're tied to the rails.

"I would need time with the kids," Steve said. "Real time. Yesterday, I rented a house."

Now Gretchen was on it; she had no choice.

"Is this somewhere you expect to bring the kids?" she said.

"Yes," Steve said.

"Then I think you should have brought this up with me before you actually rented it. I want to sign off on any place the kids are going to be," Gretchen said.

"I'd like you to come and see it," Steve said.

"Where is this place?" Gretchen said.

"In the avenues," Steve said. "Forty-first at Lawton."

That brought Gretchen up straight in her chair.

"That's miles away from my apartment," she said.

"It's fifteen minutes away, less without traffic," Steve said.

The avenues was one of the quietest parts of the city, completely unhip. Lots of Asian families, lots of middle-class kids. Low crime, low charm, bad restaurants.

"I don't get it," Gretchen said. Sandy thought Gretchen didn't get it because she didn't understand that she'd unleashed a new Steve.

"It's got a backyard where the kids can play, a playground within a few blocks," Steve said. "We could do things there. Projects. There's room."

Gretchen cut him off: "What's going on?" she said in an even, angry tone.

"I need a place where I can actually take care of the kids, not camp out with them every couple of weeks," Steve said.

"Are you talking about changing our agreement concerning the kids?" Gretchen said, her voice low. "Because that is a very serious thing."

Sandy let them roll with it.

"I realize that," Steve said.

"What do you want?" Gretchen said.

"I want to be a real part of my kids' lives," Steve said. "I'd like to work this out so that they spend a week with me, a week with you. I'm not sure about the details, but that's what I'd like."

He was looking at her intently.

Gretchen shut her eyes. You see it, don't you, Sandy thought. Her eyes opened.

"I can't believe you're doing this to me," she said slowly. She looked over at Sandy, as if she expected help. Sandy didn't have any to give.

"Now you think you're going to take over the kids?" Gretchen said.

"That's the last thing I want to do," Steve said. "I just want to have a real role in their lives."

He leaned forward. Looked pleadingly at Gretchen.

"I've given this a lot of thought. I've realized that everything is connected. When you pull one string, everything falls apart, and you have to put everything back together in a different way," Steve said. "I need to have real time with the kids, to do that I need a real home and I need a different relationship with work."

Gretchen looked at Sandy again. Then back at Steve.

"You want the kids for a week?" Gretchen said. "You don't even know how to cook."

"I'll learn. How hard can it be?"

"Bill said you might do something like this," Gretchen said. "When you found out I was going to spend a weekend with him."

"This has absolutely nothing to do with that. This has

to do with what has been happening here, in this room. The conversations here made me realize that I needed to change."

"So now, after all this time, you've decided that you want to have a real role in the kids' lives," Gretchen said hard and dangerously. "I actually didn't see this coming. I knew it was out there, I knew it was possible, but I didn't think you'd do it. When is this change supposed to occur?"

"I'm getting the place painted, and I need to buy some furniture," Steve said. "I can get that done within a week. I'm pushing everyone hard."

"I want to see this place," Gretchen said.

"I'll show it to you anytime you want," Steve said.

"If you don't mind, I'd like to go see it alone," Gretchen said. "If you could give me the exact address and loan me a key?"

"Sure," Steve said.

Now Gretchen turned back to Sandy for the third time.

"You haven't said anything, Sandy," Gretchen said.

"I think Steve is right about this," Sandy said. "In the long run, it's going to be better for the kids, and it's also part of the process of you guys separating."

"You think it's better for the kids to switch houses every week? You think that?" Gretchen said.

"In this case. With you two. Yes. I think that," Sandy said.

Gretchen shook her head. She looked down at her lap, then up again.

"I'm feeling very, very sad," Gretchen said.

Now she looked at Steve.

"Sandy calls this a step in separating, but you realize that she really means we're going straight toward a divorce, don't you?" Gretchen said.

"That's not what I mean," Sandy said. "Separating is necessary if you are ever going to get back together. That may sound illogical, but it's true. And Steve taking responsibility for the children is part of separating."

"That is psychobabble," Gretchen said.

Sandy let it go. Right now, Gretchen was beyond reasoning with.

"Why do you think we're heading straight for a divorce?" Steve said.

"You're probably thinking because this has made me so angry with you, I'm going to divorce you, but it's not that," Gretchen said. "It's because we're learning how to divorce. Sandy is teaching us not to kill each other in the divorce process, and now we'll learn how to schedule the children, how to plan their activities so they fit into our respective weeks. How to make sure that we've packed the clothes and the homework when we make the weekly transition. How to say goodbye to the kids each week without freaking them out. How to pretend that we respect each other so that the kids don't go psychotic when they're teenagers."

"We're not getting divorced," Steve said. "We are not getting divorced."

"As if you make the decisions. Actually, you'll probably be the one who files, you'll have your new house and new life. Or maybe I'll make it easy for you and die," Gretchen said.

At this moment, Gretchen reminded Sandy of a beautiful serpent, wound up, coiled, glistening head thrown back, ready to strike. Did Steve see that?

"If this doesn't work, we can change it," Steve said.

"It hurts too much," Gretchen said. "I can't play these games. If this is what you want, then this is it."

Suddenly Gretchen stood up.

"I know there is time left, but I'm completely exhausted, just gone. I'm going home. We can pick this up next week." She grabbed her coat and purse.

"Okay," Sandy said. "I'll see you next week."

Gretchen turned back at the door.

"Leave the key and the directions to your new place at my apartment, will you?" she said to Steve.

And then she was gone. Steve and Sandy sat together for a few minutes, both taking it in. Finally Sandy broke the spell.

"How do you feel about this, Steve?" Sandy asked.

"I'm sad too," Steve said. "I think she's right. We're learning how to divorce. Before, when the kids would camp out at my apartment every other weekend, it was like we were playing a game called separation. But now it's not a game. I'm not sure we can go back."

"You can't go back," Sandy said. "And you don't want to."

Steve looked at Sandy with feeling.

"Actually, you're right, I don't want to go back," Steve said. "I treated our marriage as if it were a game. I've made some terrible mistakes."

"Why do you think Gretchen is feeling so sad?" Sandy asked.

"She said why. Because she thinks we're going to get a divorce," Steve said.

"And why does that make her so sad?" Sandy said.

She watched Steve as he thought it over, taking his time.

"I guess we had a lot of dreams and it's sad to give them up," Steve said. "She thought we would have this happy family and these wonderful kids and we'd all be together. And I let her down."

"That's right," Sandy said. "That's what Gretchen is feeling. I notice that you didn't mention Bill. Why not? She just spent the weekend with him."

"You think she's thinking about Bill?" Steve asked. It had caught him by surprise. Was she? he seemed to wonder, now that Sandy had brought it up.

"No, I don't think so," Sandy said. "But what else is she thinking?"

"Maybe she's also feeling scared," Steve said. "I know I'm scared. This whole damn stuff is terrifying."

"That's right," Sandy said. "She's feeling scared. Terrified. What else?"

"I'm not sure," Steve said.

"Maybe she's feeling left behind," Sandy suggested.

"I need to be very careful," Steve said cautiously.

Sandy wondered exactly what he meant. That he needed to be careful of Gretchen, that in her fear, she might be capable of anything? That he needed to be careful of the little spark of hope and even love that still existed between them, to make sure that it didn't get blown out in these big, dark winds?

10.

Sandy noticed: There was no deep-throated glug-glug. No boom-boom rumble. Steve came into the room to join Sandy and Gretchen unannounced, without car fanfare.

"Where's your car?" Gretchen asked Steve.

"I sold it," Steve said. "I now own a Subaru Outback. It's sitting in the lot next to your Prius. The Outback is the vehicle of choice among the preschool crowd. Four-wheel drive. You can take it to the snow."

Gretchen shot him a look.

"I want to know before you take the kids anywhere," she said.

"Of course," Steve said.

Steve had had his first week alone with the kids, in his new house. Now they were back with Gretchen.

"Did you take the kids somewhere?" Gretchen asked evenly.

"No, we pretty much stayed in the city," Steve answered.

"Pretty much?" Gretchen said. "What does that mean?"

"We went to Ocean Beach," Steve said. "We went to the children's playground in the park and they rode the carousel. We went to a couple of playgrounds actually."

"I guess Chris was talking about the carousel," Gretchen said. "Only, he called it the up-and-down. I had no idea what he meant."

"That's what he calls the carousel," Steve said. "Because the animals go up and down."

"Anyway, if you're going to take them somewhere during your week, I'd like to know about it beforehand," Gretchen said.

"So are we talking like going out to Stinson Beach?" Steve said. "Going to Napa? If I was taking them overnight somewhere, of course I'd tell you. But if I was taking them to the Santa Cruz boardwalk? Would you like me to tell you about that?"

"Why can't you both share your plans for the weeks

you have the kids?" Sandy said. "Why is it such a loaded question?"

They both paused, thinking.

"We should do that," Steve said finally.

"But you don't, do you?" Sandy said. "I wonder why."

"We've only just started this week-on, week-off system," Gretchen said. "Come on."

"You've been dealing with sharing the kids for three months though," Sandy said. "Why aren't you talking to each other?"

"We are talking to each other," Gretchen said.

"Oh, come on," Sandy said. She looked at Steve. "Did you call Gretchen the whole week that you had the kids?"

"No," Steve said.

"Why not?" Sandy said. "Would you have called her if you were taking the kids to Santa Cruz?"

"This was Gretchen's alone time," Steve said. "I didn't want to bother her."

"I want you to bother her," Sandy said. "But I don't think it was about that. I think you were worried that Gretchen might be with some other guy."

That brought Steve up in his chair.

"I guess I don't want any surprises," Steve said.

"Can we go back to how we're going to handle the kids?" Gretchen said.

Sandy let the moment pass, thinking she'd dropped a few land mines that would explode later.

"Sure," she said.

"I don't want any surprises from Steve when he has the kids a whole week," Gretchen said.

"Okay," Steve said. "With that thought, I signed the kids up for a class at the Academy of Sciences. Is that okay?"

"And I want to know before you sign them up for anything," Gretchen said.

"They haven't started the class yet," Steve said. "It was on a first-come, first-served basis, so I had to sign them up to give them a chance to take it. But if you don't like it, I can cancel."

"What is the course?" Gretchen said.

"Pottery," Steve said.

"You don't think they might be a little young for that?" Gretchen said.

"They don't throw pots," Steve said. "They just mess around with clay."

He smiled.

"What are you grinning for?" Gretchen said.

"You're going to make fun of me," Steve said. "But I'm taking cooking lessons. Italian cooking."

Sandy noticed: Steve was almost cocky. He was in a good mood for a change. Was it the cooking lessons, maybe? Who was the teacher?

Gretchen raised her hands up, palms toward Sandy, meaning, What are we doing here?

"Are we going to discuss anything today? Is there anything on the agenda?" Gretchen said to her.

"I think we've been discussing important things," Sandy said. "But is there something on your mind?"

"One thing is that I don't want to waste my time here," Gretchen said. "I have limited time and limited money."

Sandy thought, We took care of the money the first time you were in this office. What is it, Gretchen?

"What are you thinking about time and money?" Sandy said.

"I'm thinking that maybe our work here is done," Gretchen said. "I've agreed that Steve can have the kids half the time. We have a schedule. What else is there to discuss?"

"I think a lot," Sandy said.

"I can see that this has been helpful for Steve," Gretchen said. "He's made some changes that he needed to make. That's good. But as for me, I don't need to know about Steve's cooking lessons. What's in it for me to spend my time here at this point?"

"Why don't you want to know about Steve's cooking lessons?" Sandy said. "I do. I wonder if he has some beautiful Italian woman coming over to teach him."

"That's just what I don't want to know," Gretchen said.

"Why not?" Sandy said. "Who is teaching you to cook, Steve?"

"A chef," Steve said.

"And the chef's name?" Sandy asked.

"Gabrielle," Steve said.

Gretchen shot a look at Sandy as if to ask, Are you evil?

"All of this just makes me sad," Gretchen said.

"If I'm understanding you correctly, you're saying something like this: We've done a pretty good job working out the practical issues of living separately. The next step would be working on getting to really understand each other, to learn new ways to deal with each other, and you don't want to do that," Sandy said.

"Yes, that's what I mean," Gretchen said. "You were big on how we needed to separate. Well, now we are finally separated. I don't see what else we need to learn. Why do I need to know more about Steve and me?"

"Can I ask if you're happy?" Sandy said. "That's sort of the bottom line here, I think."

"No, I'm not happy," Gretchen said. "I have trouble sleeping. I miss the kids really badly when I don't have them. So, no. Honestly, I'm not happy. But I think having these meetings with Steve just makes me feel worse."

"Why is that, do you think?" Sandy said. She was looking at Gretchen, but from the corner of her eye she saw Steve. He was staring at Gretchen transfixed, as if his life were hanging in the balance.

Sandy looked at the green chair. She felt something there, sitting there, watching.

"On the one hand, these changes in Steve, I don't really believe them," Gretchen said. "I think they're an act. On the other hand, if they are real, then it makes me incredibly sad, because we might have made a life together if Steve had made these changes long ago."

Gretchen turned in her chair and looked at Steve.

"I wish I could feel something for you, but I can't," she said. "It just isn't there, Steve. You stamped it out and it's not coming back. I can never trust you again."

Tears formed in the corners of Gretchen's beautiful blue eyes.

"I'm so sorry," Steve said in a whisper.

"So am I," Gretchen said.

The land mine went off.

She started to get up, saying, "I think that's it for me. Thanks for working with us, Sandy."

"This is just the beginning," Sandy said forcefully. "You are absolutely crazy if you walk out of here now. I mean it. I understand how badly you feel, but you're going to feel much worse if you leave." Sandy got halfway out of her chair: "Sit down!"

It was as if Sandy had shot Gretchen in the chest with an arrow. Gretchen fell back into her seat and her eyes filled with tears; she cried, weeping in gasps. Sandy reached for the box of tissues on the end table near her chair and held it out for Gretchen. But Gretchen wasn't ready for it. Her eyes were closed and she was sobbing in big gulps of air. It took almost five minutes before she shook it off, opened her eyes. Then Sandy handed her the box, and this time she took a tissue.

"Wow, I'm really, really tired," Gretchen said. "I'm a wreck. I slept maybe twenty minutes last night."

She blinked, looked around, coming back to the room.

"I wonder if I can have a session alone with you,"

Gretchen said to Sandy. "I have things to say that I'm not comfortable saying with Steve around."

"Sure," Sandy said.

Gretchen looked over at Steve.

"Don't let this freak you out, this isn't about you or us," Gretchen said.

How much of this did Steve understand? Sandy wondered. He didn't respond to Gretchen, but he seemed relieved, as if his world had spun around on a roulette wheel, he had bet on the red, and amazingly the little bouncing ball had landed there, on the red, in a safe place for now.

11.

First Gretchen left a session in the middle of it, then she tried to stop altogether. What was going on? Gretchen was seeing something up ahead that she didn't want to face, some terrible problem. What is it, Gretchen? Sandy wondered.

"I'm sorry I lost it the other day," Gretchen said.

"Something important is going on," Sandy said. "You didn't want to stop our sessions because all the problems had been solved between you and Steve."

"Look, I can't keep going on this way," Gretchen said, leaning forward. "I was really excited and energized when I separated from Steve and moved into the city. Now I'm drained, exhausted. This whole process is killing me. I can't keep going through it."

She sounded drained, exhausted.

"Can we talk a little about what you're going through?" Sandy said.

"So there is Bill back in L.A., who I've been talking to on the phone pretty much every day for months, but with whom I've actually gotten together four times in all," Gretchen said. "The fact is he's married, it's his second marriage. Suppose we could work out the logistical issues. Would I want to be this guy's third wife?"

This guy? Sandy didn't say anything.

"I'm so lonely, I've actually made some other stupid choices, and recently slept with someone that I regret," Gretchen said.

She sort of threw her hands in the air, rolled her eyes.

"Oh, I don't know," she said. "I don't know if I regret it. I mean, so what?"

"Right," Sandy said.

"But I want more out of life. I feel like I'm going round and round and round, while Steve is making some sort of crazy progress," Gretchen said. "I'm losing it."

"You look really tired," Sandy said.

"I look like shit," Gretchen said.

But actually, though she did look tired, in some ways

Gretchen seemed more beautiful than ever. What is it, Sandy wondered, what's got you scared?

"No, you just look tired," Sandy said.

"I don't sleep, I forget stuff, I'm winging it when I'm teaching. I'm really unhappy," Gretchen said.

"I'm sorry," Sandy said.

"I have to tell you," Gretchen said. "One reason that I regret sleeping with this guy is that now he won't leave me alone. He got the idea that somehow I like him."

"He got lucky," Sandy said. "But he didn't get that lucky."

"I feel trapped," Gretchen said. "Like I'm being tossed all over the place."

"Tell me more," Sandy said. Anything to keep Gretchen talking.

"I'm feeling trapped, no options, no way forward. You know, I haven't met a single guy who I would want to be with except for Bill, and as I said, that is really, really wearing thin," Gretchen said.

"Why?" Sandy said.

"It isn't enough to talk to him on the telephone," Gretchen said. "It just isn't working for me anymore."

"When you do talk on the phone, how do you feel?" Sandy asked.

"I used to tell him everything, he was like my spirit guide. He'd been through all of this before. Now it's different," Gretchen said.

"Like how?" Sandy asked.

"I'm not sure," Gretchen said slowly.

"I have an idea of what may be going on," Sandy said. "Maybe the issues you're facing now are ones that Bill can't help you with. You're still married. He's an expert on divorce."

"Haven't they been the same issues all along?" Gretchen said.

"For three months, we dealt with the practical issues of separating. Steve had to get to the point of seeing he needed his own place. You had to accept Steve taking equal care of the kids. The big issue left is seeing if you can develop skills so that you can relate to each other in a much better way," Sandy said.

"I don't want to live with Steve again," Gretchen said.

"I'm sorry, but I don't believe you," Sandy said. "Everything I'm hearing says the other options aren't appealing. Bill isn't the right guy. The guy you slept with isn't right. Who do you think about the most? It's Steve. Isn't it?"

"I can't fucking get rid of him," Gretchen hissed.

"I know you can't," Sandy said. "Because you're not done with him. You still have issues with Steve."

"Maybe, but if I really need to, I will. I'll get the best, most hard-ass lawyer and sue him for divorce," Gretchen said.

"The last thing you want is a lawyer, isn't it?" Sandy said.

"Of course, I hate them, I hate the idea of them,"

Gretchen said, her temper rising with her voice. "But I'm not going to be pushed around."

"So what you were really saying is that if Steve hurts you, then you'll get a lawyer and sue him," Sandy said.

"Maybe," Gretchen said. "I don't know."

"Can I ask you one thing?" Sandy said.

Gretchen nodded. "Of course," she said.

"How do you really feel about Steve right now?"

"I don't know, I don't know," Gretchen said, her hands up, palms facing Sandy. "I honestly do not know. I'd like him to suffer, but he seems to be immune to suffering. He seems to always land on his feet."

"Oh, he's suffered," Sandy said. "He still is."

"I doubt it," Gretchen said.

"Steve hurt you so much that you don't know if you can live with him again. But if somehow you could begin to create a relationship that transcended all that hurt, all the suffering, and Steve kept changing before your eyes . . ."

"That's a lot of ifs," Gretchen said.

"But much of it is under your control," Sandy said. "Why don't you give it time and see what happens?"

"Why does Steve constantly get what he wants?" Gretchen said angrily. "He doesn't support my work, he ignores the kids, he's an egomaniac, he screws around behind my back. Do you understand that he cheated on me when I was crazed about getting tenure? He fucked some bimbo. Then he gets me to take him back? How does he deserve that?"

"I can never figure out who deserves what," Sandy said. "But if you're saying that Steve would be incredibly lucky to get back together with you, yes, he would be."

Gretchen leaned toward Sandy conspiratorially.

"I have something funny to tell you," she said. "You remember Bonny?"

"I don't think you told me about Bonny," Sandy said.

"She went to college with me and Steve, has two children, is divorced, and has been an important friend. Sort of," Gretchen said.

Oh yes, I know all about you, Bonny, Sandy thought, pretty sure of what was coming.

"She asked me what I would think if she went out with Steve," Gretchen said. She rolled her eyes.

"What did you tell her?" Sandy said.

"I said it's none of my business," Gretchen said. "You're welcome to him."

"How do you really feel?" Sandy said.

"I really feel like I took Steve apart and put him back together again as the new Steve, and now Bonny gets him?"

"That's funny," Sandy said.

"It's ironic, isn't it?" Gretchen said.

"Have they gone out together?" Sandy asked.

"How would I know?" Gretchen said.

"One way would be to ask Steve," Sandy said.

"I don't want to know about Steve's personal life," Gretchen said.

Sandy shook her head.

"You have these sorts of rules," Sandy said. "Or maybe they're walls. Can I ask you why you don't want to know about Steve's personal life? And it doesn't work for me if you say, I don't have any right to know about Steve's love life. No rights and wrongs."

"It's his private life," Gretchen said exasperatedly.

"So what?" Sandy said. "What difference does that make?"

"I don't want to tell him about my private life," Gretchen said.

"So what?" Sandy said. "We're not talking about you telling Steve about your lovers. We're talking about him telling you about his."

"Isn't there a quid pro quo?" Gretchen said. "If I ask him about his private life, doesn't he have the right to ask about mine?"

"No," Sandy said. "No rights."

"Okay," Gretchen said. "No rights. But he'll presume that I won't mind if he asks me."

"Then you can straighten him out," Sandy said. "You can just say, I don't feel comfortable talking with you about my love life. I only want to talk about yours."

"You think that will work with Steve?" Gretchen said. She was incredulous, and suddenly she smiled. "Sandy, you are sort of nuts," she added.

Yes, Sandy thought. I've been told that. She looked at the green chair, then back at Gretchen, who noticed.

"What's with the green chair?" Gretchen asked. "It doesn't match the other chairs."

"I think it does," Sandy said.

Gretchen shrugged and didn't pursue it.

"Why wouldn't it work with Steve?" Sandy said. "Really. Seriously. Why can't you have things the way you want them? Especially with Steve: just tell him what you want. Frankly, that's pretty much all you've got to do. But you don't do it."

Gretchen looked off toward the corner of the room.

"Okay, let me ask you something else. If Steve tells you he wants to talk to you about going out with Bonny, what are you going to do?" Sandy said.

"Tell him it's none of my business," Gretchen said. "I can't stop him from going out with someone."

"I don't believe that for a second," Sandy said. "You can stop Steve in a heartbeat."

Gretchen considered it again.

"Yes. I could," she said. "I could."

"Of course you could," Sandy said. "What I don't understand is why there are all these rules about what you talk to Steve about. If I were you, and Bonny had asked if she could sleep with my husband, I think I'd talk to him about it."

"She didn't ask if she could sleep with Steve," Gretchen said.

"Oh, come on," Sandy said. "What do you think it was all about?"

"Steve and I are separated," Gretchen said.

"Again, so what? Are you divorced? And even if you were, would that make any difference?" Sandy said.

"Are you telling me that you want me to talk to Steve about what Bonny said?" Gretchen asked.

"Not quite," Sandy said. "I'm saying you'd like to talk to Steve about it, but are scared of doing it because you don't want to have any intimacy with Steve, for lots of good reasons."

"I actually agree with that," Gretchen said. "I have lots of good reasons for not talking about personal stuff with Steve. Are you saying I should anyway?"

"These are complicated feelings, what you're going through with Steve. Yes, I think you have to engage with him if you're ever going to sort these feelings out, and that doesn't mean I'm trying to get you guys back together," Sandy said. Is that true? Sandy wondered.

"I'm really, really angry with Steve," Gretchen said. "Sometimes it's a white-hot anger that burns through me and just kills."

"I think that is something you should talk to Steve about," Sandy said. She leaned toward Gretchen and took her hand. Gretchen let her hold it.

"You can do this, Gretchen," Sandy said. "You already changed Steve. That was great work. Don't stop now."

12.

"When I saw Gandy alone," Gretchen said to Steve, "I talked to her about how it made me feel that you were renting the house, that you were taking the kids half-time."

Taking was an interesting word choice . . .

"Okay," Steve said.

"I've come to terms with the fact that I can't stop you from taking them half-time," Gretchen said. "I will also say that the house you've rented is fine. It has a lot of space. I like the yard. It's quiet."

"I'm glad you like it," Steve said.

"Another thing that I told Sandy was that Bonny Garvey asked me if I would be upset with her if she went out with you," Gretchen said. "I told her that we were separated and it was up to you to decide who you wanted to go out with."

"I went out with Bonny once, and I don't plan on seeing her again," Steve said. "But thanks for telling me. Anything else you need to tell me?"

"That's it," Gretchen said.

"That was a pretty lame conversation," Sandy said.

There was more about Bonny, both of them knew it, both of them didn't want to talk about it. Sandy decided to deal with it.

"You guys really need to do better," Sandy said. "It's so important. Everything is flat, affectless. It's all so formal. Gretchen, you didn't have any feelings when Bonny told you she was interested in Steve? That's not what you told me."

"I told you it wasn't my business who Steve went out with," Gretchen said.

"That was just one of the things you said," Sandy said. She leaned toward Gretchen. "We need to take some chances here, talk about your emotions. What did you feel when Bonny talked to you, Gretchen?"

"I don't know," Gretchen said. "I guess I thought it was inevitable. Bonny is divorced, she's always liked Steve."

"Again, that is a statement of fact," Sandy said. "How did it make you feel?"

Gretchen shook her head.

"Okay, I guess it pissed me off," she said.

"Why?"

"I force these changes in Steve—he becomes superdad—and someone else gets the benefits?" Gretchen said. She crossed her arms. "And I also feel sad, because this separation is moving on, and on, and on toward divorce. There goes that dream I had a long time ago, the one that Steve ruined."

"I feel sad too," Steve said.

But it wasn't moving on and on toward divorce, not at the moment anyway, Sandy thought. Gretchen? She seemed to think it had to move to divorce. It was the way her mind went. Again with the rules. But, they were talking.

Sandy decided to leave Bonny Garvey until later.

"That's better," Sandy said. "Now let's try something else. I'd like you both to talk to each other and let me listen in. I'm not going to direct the conversation, I'm just going to observe."

Steve and Gretchen looked at each other, they looked at Sandy, then back at each other. Then Gretchen looked at Steve, hard.

"For a long time, I've felt as if, when I try to say something and it runs counter to whatever you believe, you immediately have arguments ready for me," Gretchen said.

She was still looking intently at Steve.

"You're ready for me, like you're lurking, waiting to hit me with your arguments," Gretchen said. "Do you understand how much that turns me off?"

Steve looked at Sandy, and she looked back at him but didn't say anything. He looked at Gretchen.

"I feel as if you are mad all the time," Steve said. "As if you're always attacking me, always angry with me. Nothing is . . ."

"Hold on. We didn't get very far," Sandy said forcefully.

She looked at Steve. "Steve, Gretchen tells you something and you don't respond to it. Gretchen talked first. She went out on a limb there. And you didn't say a word about what she said. You just changed the subject so that it was about her doing stuff that hurt you."

Steve looked at Sandy as if he didn't understand what she was saying.

"I told her how I felt about it," he said.

"No, you told her that she was mad all the time," Sandy said. "You didn't even acknowledge what she'd said. It's like this, Steve."

Sandy leaned forward in her chair, she moved her hands as if she was wrapping something up.

"Like Gretchen says, I fell and I'm bleeding. And you look at her and say, You'll live. I want to talk about how I'm having a problem with your griping all the time. Do you understand that you did that, Steve?"

Steve looked at Sandy with an almost frightened look of incomprehension.

"Not really," Steve said. "I thought we were talking about what was wrong with our relationship."

"Steve," Sandy said. "I said I wanted to listen in on a conversation between you and Gretchen. What happened?"

"Gretchen said that whenever she says something I always have arguments ready to support my side," Steve said.

"Yes," Sandy said. "And then you said?"

"That Gretchen was always mad at me," Steve said.

"Someone had to start this conversation I asked for. You could have, but you didn't. So Gretchen did. And when she did, you ignored her and changed the subject."

Sandy shook her head. Both Steve and Gretchen read it for what it said: How do I get Steve to understand?

"Actually, Steve, the more I think about it, you let her start it and you were ready to jump on her," Sandy said. "As Gretchen said, you were waiting for her. Listen, I want you to think about what Gretchen says to you."

"I do," Steve said, pushing it out, not angry but defensive.

"Well, maybe I said it wrong," Sandy said. "I want you to listen to what Gretchen said and then you need to respond to what she said. Never change the subject."

"I didn't change the subject," Steve said.

He is a very smart guy; how much money did his

education cost? And he doesn't think he changed the subject?

"We were talking about what was wrong with our relationship," Steve said quietly, carefully, and scared. "I kept on that theme."

Sandy looked over at Gretchen. It was amusing. There was a faint half smile on Gretchen's face, just visible.

"No," Sandy said. "The theme was Gretchen. That was the theme. You went somewhere else. Gretchen was talking about what Gretchen thinks is wrong with the relationship. Gretchen put it out there. She was willing to start the conversation. The minute she said, Here is the problem, when she said, There is a problem with you, you said, No: the problem is with you, let's talk about you.

"You know what I think, Steve? You don't want to talk about your relationship with Gretchen. It scares you. You're scared of what Gretchen will say, so you try to shut her down."

Steve nodded.

"Can I try it again?" Steve asked.

"Sure," Sandy said.

Steve turned to Gretchen.

"You feel as if I'm waiting to jump all over you when you say something personal," Steve said. "And you said that really makes you angry."

"I don't know about angry," Gretchen said. "It makes me feel desperate."

"Why desperate?" Steve asked.

"Like I can't be my real self, I have to be this pretend self," Gretchen said. "See how we got in trouble? I needed someone who would listen to me, just listen. Steve, most of the time, I would be grateful if you never even said a word. Can you do that?"

13.

"*We're not getting anywhere,*" Sandy said. "Let's start this over. You called and wanted to see me alone, and what you want to talk over with me, I think I've finally got this right, is whether you need to be completely honest with Gretchen in these sessions. Is that it?"

"What I was trying to say is that there are different levels of truth," Steve said. "I can tell Gretchen absolutely everything, I can leave some things out that perhaps I'm not ready to talk about, or I could actually lie to her."

"I have no idea how to deal with what you just said to me," Sandy said. "Because it seems to me that the issue needs to be approached in a different way. Look, Steve, do you mind if I just talk? That we don't have a dialogue?"

"Sure," Steve said. "Of course."

"First of all, I'm really glad you called and asked to see me, because this is so important. The question is, What kind of a life do you want to live? Do you want to live one where you know what is going on? Or where you don't? Do you want a life where you make rational decisions because you know the facts, or where you make guesses? This question is more important than whether you get back together with Gretchen or don't get back together. Let me tell you a story."

Sandy settled back in her chair.

"My parents got divorced when I was about twelve. There were lots of reasons for their divorce. My mother was well on her way to becoming an important real estate developer and didn't have a lot of time for my dad, but at its core the basic problem was that my mother lived in a world where everything was just great, it was fine, there were no troubles. But of course there were troubles, it was just that no one was allowed to talk about them. Well, that didn't work well for my dad, because he had troubles, who doesn't, and he wanted to talk about them. So the two of them drifted away from each other and ultimately my dad found someone who would listen to him. But me, I was still stuck with my mother, who was telling me that everything was for the best, the divorce was a good thing, and weren't we so lucky and happy?

"Well, I wasn't feeling lucky or happy. I was feeling miserable, but I couldn't say that to my mom, she just wouldn't hear it, so you know what I did? I mean, I was thinking I might have to commit suicide to show Mom the real state of affairs, but that didn't seem like such a good idea, since I'd end up dead. So what did I do? I called a cab and went to my dad's. I had to be in a place where the reality of the world corresponded with my own personal reality. My mother tried to make me come home, she threatened in every way she could. She blamed my dad, saying that he had obviously planned this. But give him credit. He stood up to her. Anyway, what happened was that I ended up spending my entire high school years with my father."

Sandy shrugged.

"Baseline reality is probably the most important thing in the world," she said. "So I think you need to tell Gretchen everything that's going on, everything. And if there is something you don't want to tell her, something you are scared to tell her, that is exactly what you need to tell her. Do you think you can do that?"

"But the problem is that if I tell Gretchen I slept with Bonny Garvey, for instance, she will divorce me," Steve said.

"I doubt it," Sandy said. "Just to give you a reality check, she could have divorced you months ago. I thought she would. She didn't. Why? I think she's looking for you to change. Why don't you try it?"

"I am trying," Steve said defensively.

"I don't mean taking the kids half-time, that was the easy part," Sandy said.

Steve looked annoyed, as if Sandy didn't understand what he was saying.

"Yes, I agree that I need to begin to tell Gretchen the truth, always," Steve said. "But I don't get why I need to go back and tell her everything I've ever done wrong. I'd like a fresh start."

"There is no fresh start," Sandy said evenly. "Gretchen will never forget anything. Can we deal with reality?"

"Is there forgiveness?" Steve asked.

"How could she forgive something she doesn't know about?" Sandy said. "Why don't we deal with Bonny."

"There's one thing more," Steve said. "Bonny invited me to take my kids up to her parents' place in Napa, where they would play with her kids. A weekend away."

"Why did Bonny ask you to take the kids up to her folks' place in Napa for the weekend?" Sandy asked.

"I don't know. She wanted company?" Steve said. "She was lonely?"

"Oh, Steve," Sandy said. "Look, she knows it will drive Gretchen crazy. She wants to split you guys up permanently."

Steve looked at Sandy with confusion.

"Steve, think about it," Sandy said. "Bonny asked

Gretchen if it was okay to go out with you, because she wants Gretchen to know she's going out with you. Next thing she's going to do is let Gretchen know that she's sleeping with you."

"I don't think she would do that," Steve said.

"Of course she would," Sandy said. "And why not? So the question is, Who do you want Gretchen to hear this from? You? Or Bonny?"

Steve stared at Sandy.

"Of course Gretchen *knows* you slept with Bonny," Sandy said. "She has just ignored it, since it hasn't been thrown right in her face. Gretchen is very good at ignoring unpleasant realities. It's one of her big problems, but she's working on it."

"I should never have slept with Bonny," Steve said. "I knew it at the time."

"All this moral stuff," Sandy said. "You both should take vows. Should, shouldn't. Steve, you were as lonely as you'd ever been. Your wife had thrown you out. She was in love with someone else. So you looked for someone to comfort you. Anyone would."

"Right," Steve said. "And you think that's what Gretchen is going to think? That I was just really lonely?"

"What do you think she's going to think?" Sandy said.

"That I'm a liar. A cheat. That I went to bed with one of her best friends," Steve said.

"You're so melodramatic," Sandy said. "I mean, yes, technically you *are* a liar and a cheat, but everyone makes mistakes. After Gretchen gets over her first reaction. Yes, anger is her first reaction. But when she has some emotional space, a little time, what is she going to feel?"

"I'm going to be late-middle-aged by the time she's not angry," Steve said.

"Come on," Sandy said. "As a matter of fact, Gretchen is doing much better in the anger management department, which I hope you've noticed. No, really think about this: What is she going to feel?"

"I don't know," Steve said.

"Okay, let's go back to square one," Sandy said. "Your son, Chris, he hits his little sister. What does Gretchen feel?"

"I guess disappointed," Steve said. "She's teaching him to use his words."

"So by analogy?"

"Gretchen is going to feel disappointed in me?"

"Of course," Sandy said. "One of Gretchen's most important projects in life has been making you better, making you into a better person. She's tried and tried. Only, she keeps failing. You know why?"

"I'm a slow learner?" Steve said.

Sandy ignored the joke and looked hard at Steve.

"Because you perceive her efforts as criticism," Sandy said. "She's trying to make you better, but all she's managed to do is make you angry and set you up to cheat on her because your feelings are hurt and you feel unloved."

"I have to think about this," Steve said slowly.

"She's a teacher," Sandy said, smiling slightly. "If you could only realize that her goal is to make you better, to teach you, not to hurt you, you would be so much better off."

"So she's going to feel disappointed with me because I slept with Bonny?" Steve said.

"I think you can count on it," Sandy said. "If you're going to sleep with someone, at least do it with someone Gretchen respects."

"That's funny," Steve said.

"Yeah?" Sandy said. "Why is it funny?"

"That's what I thought myself," Steve said. "Afterward, I thought, This is crazy, you don't even respect her."

"There you go," Sandy said. "So you need to tell Gretchen about it."

"You really think it's going to be okay?" Steve said.

"Probably not, but I don't know," Sandy said. "I do know it's better than waiting for Bonny to do it. Bonny is part of your circle of friends. Of course Gretchen needs to know about it. By the way, are you still sleeping with Bonny?"

"No," Steve said. "I only slept with her once."

"Sometime we should talk about Gabrielle," Sandy said.

"Gabrielle?"

"Just think about it," Sandy said. "Then we'll talk."

"You're a terrifying marriage counselor," Steve said.

Sandy honed in on Steve, looked right into his eyes.

"Play the long game, Steve," she said.

14.

Steve was looking better. His skin had some shine in it, he moved more athletically now.

"I want to discuss something with you," Gretchen said. It came out a bit formally, an announcement that she expected Steve to pay attention. "I talked to you about this a while back, but there was stuff I skipped."

"Okay," Steve said.

"Remember when Bonny asked me if it was all right with me if she went out with you?" Gretchen said.

She got Steve's full attention, Sandy noticed. It was great: they were both on the same page emotionally, the same thing bothering them. But now they were . . . Were they? They were at least trying to go further.

"I told her that who you went out with wasn't any of my business," Gretchen said.

Steve nodded.

"But when I really think about it, I do care who you go out with," Gretchen said.

Gretchen had Sandy's attention too, her full attention, just like Steve. It was unlike Gretchen to wade into the water on her own. Usually, she needed to be pushed.

"For one thing, I don't want the kids hanging out with someone I don't trust," Gretchen said. "For another, I do have some lingering affection for you. I'm nervous telling you this, because I think you're going to make too much of it."

"I have affection for you too," Steve said.

This talk about mutual affection was enough to tip Steve into the danger zone, the place where Sandy wanted him. Sandy could see it on his face. He brightened. He hoped.

"Bonny invited me to take the kids up to her folks' place in Napa for a weekend when I had the kids," Steve said. "I told her it might be fun to come up there for the day but that I wasn't going to spend the weekend."

Gretchen didn't say anything. Sandy could feel the wheels spinning in her brain, though.

"Why did you tell her that you wouldn't spend the weekend?" Sandy said.

"I wondered, What would I think if Gretchen did this with some divorced guy who had children? Went away for the weekend with all their kids?" Steve said. "It would freak me out. And not because they were having sex together. Not even because they had sex with the kids in the next bedroom. Because I would think that Gretchen was trying to replace me."

"If you have sex with the kids in the next room, I'll kill you," Gretchen said evenly, all the screws on her diving suit clamping down. She was diving toward the bottom.

"It's not going to happen," Steve said.

"Well, something is going to happen," Gretchen said loudly. "At some point everything is going to happen. Let's not kid ourselves. Are you crazy?"

They were, a bit, Sandy thought. Who wouldn't be?

"Talking about what happened here, just now," Sandy said. "You guys were having a pretty good conversation and then it blew up. Why? What are you feeling, Gretchen?"

"I don't know," Gretchen said.

"Of course you do," Sandy said.

"Sandy, it is such a cliché to ask, What are you feeling? It is pathetic," Gretchen said. "You keep asking, What are you feeling? I feel nothing."

Does she even know what she's saying? No, she doesn't, Sandy thought.

"Yes, I do keep asking what you are feeling," Sandy said. "Because you hide it. You hide it all the time."

They looked at each other. Gretchen had been trained to hide her feelings since she was a little kid. And Gretchen knew it. What was she supposed to do about that? She looked at Sandy as if saying, Fuck you. She didn't get that what was important was that Steve understood that she had been hiding her feelings since she was a little kid.

You can't change this, you were conditioned cruelly for years. But Steve wasn't. He doesn't have to change, he just has to understand.

"Okay, here it is," Gretchen said. She turned to Steve. "I can't believe that you would consider going up to Napa with Bonny even for a day, let alone a weekend."

"Bonny is one of our oldest friends," Steve said.

"Fuck you, Steve," Gretchen said. "But feel free to fuck whoever you want."

It was probably as close as Gretchen could get to expressing her central concern. It wasn't that close, but it was progress. Come on, Steve. See it.

"When did you talk to Bonny about going up to Napa?" Sandy asked Steve.

He doesn't even get the question.

"You mean, when did she ask me?" Steve said.

"Yes."

"I don't know, this week," Steve said. "Maybe Tuesday."

"I asked Bonny if she wanted to take her kids with me

and my kids to the Discovery Museum on Tuesday," Gretchen said. "But she didn't have her kids, she said. I also asked her if she wanted to come over and have dinner with me and my kids Tuesday night, thinking she might be lonely, being all alone."

"I had dinner with Bonny on Tuesday night," Steve said. "That's when she suggested that we take all the kids up to Napa over the weekend."

Everyone knew what they were talking about except Steve, but now he got it, and he saw the decision he had to make, and he sort of gathered himself and went forward, into the dark. Be brave. Do it, Sandy thought.

"I slept with Bonny on Tuesday night," Steve said. "I was lonely, feeling sorry for myself."

Gretchen shook her head. Everything stopped. Something had happened. It wasn't that Steve had slept with Bonny. That wasn't important. It was . . . Gretchen, do you get it?

It all stopped for a few moments. Gretchen looked around the room, as if she were searching for something. She looked at the green chair, paused on it. Then Gretchen got it. Sandy had been hoping that Steve would get Gretchen, understand the incredible trouble she had revealing her feelings. But it wasn't Steve, it was Gretchen who made a leap.

"These things happen," Gretchen said. "Believe me, I know."

"I'm sorry," Steve said.

"What do you have to be sorry for?" Gretchen said. "Sandy doesn't think much of sorry. Sad might be a better word, sad for everything that's happened. Bonny is miserable and desperate, Steve. You need to be careful. You slept with her, and the next thing, she wanted to create a blended family with you on the weekend."

Gretchen got them actually talking. Of course it hurt, but they were doing it, plowing ahead.

"It didn't make me feel good," Steve said. And hesitated. And Gretchen didn't follow up.

"Why? Why didn't it make you feel good?" Sandy said.

"I didn't feel any connection with Bonny," Steve said.

"Yeah, you did," Sandy said.

They paused again.

"You're right," Steve said. "She scared me. She told me that we had had feelings for each other since college. She was pushing me into a relationship with her. I didn't want it, but at the same time, I didn't want to hurt her."

Oh, Steve . . .

"You didn't want to hurt *her*?" Gretchen yelled. "Her? She wants you to take my kids away with her for the weekend. She knows I am going to find out about it. She expects me to explode. She's counting on me exploding. She wants to blow us up. Finish us. Don't you get it? She asks you to go away with the kids for the weekend because it will make me divorce you. And you're worried about *her* feelings?"

She got it, so much of it. So why aren't you talking more? Sandy wondered. It would make so much difference.

"Yes, I was worried, and I thought that the tiny bit of trust that we've managed to rebuild, it's all started with the kids," Steve said. "It's like they're this little island of calm we've created. And she was threatening it. I got scared and angry, and I told her to go back to her own house on Tuesday night. She didn't stay the night. I only slept with her once."

Oh, Steve, yes, you need to tell her everything, but not now and perhaps not until you're much older . . .

Gretchen looked at Sandy. "Do you think I really need to listen to this crap? I need to know how many times they made love? Why am I trying to talk to this jerk?"

Steve, Steve. Slowly. Please.

"Everything matters between you two," Sandy said to Gretchen. "He needed to tell you how many times he slept with Bonny. I don't know why. It seems cruel and stupid to me. But there is a reason. How many times matters to Steve. Why? I have no idea why he keeps score. But maybe we will find out at some point."

Sandy saw Gretchen perk up, eyes narrowed. It is the English teacher, Sandy thought, the English teacher is suddenly realizing that this character is more complicated than she had thought. Yes, Gretchen, he *keeps score*. No . . .

Suddenly Sandy realized she was wrong. Steve didn't keep score. Gretchen did.

15.

The next session, they were all over each other, as if they hadn't made any progress the session before. Sandy wasn't surprised.

"Steve, you are intolerable," Gretchen said. "And the reason is that you are a bottomless emotional pit, an emotional black hole. All you do is demand emotional attention. Nobody can handle insatiable demands like that. Gabrielle will discover it soon enough."

Gretchen was really talking about how much Steve had hurt her, how she had tried to wall him off to avoid that, and how scared she was to take the walls down.

Gabrielle?

"You were barely available for me," Steve said. "And if I did want some attention, you regarded it as selfish."

Steve didn't get it. Why would he?

Gabrielle? Something had set Gretchen off. She saw Gabrielle on the horizon.

"You made me feel as if I was pathetic for asking for any kind of intimacy," Steve said, choosing not to engage about Gabrielle.

"Your idea of intimacy was that I pay attention to you immediately when you asked for intimacy," Gretchen fumed. "But most of the time, you were in your own world. And if I asked for attention, you never gave it to me. You were so amazingly selfish."

"You never asked for anything," Steve said.

"No, you never listened," Gretchen said. "You never heard me asking."

Steve paused. He tried to think about what had happened in the past. It's not about the past, Steve, Sandy thought. She considered interrupting them, but she let them go on.

"It wasn't a good time for me," Steve said. "You know that. I was in a crazy situation. I was working twenty-five hours a day. It was like being on a runaway train. I was asking for your help so I could get off it."

"So you were like Charlie on the MTA?" Gretchen sneered. "Remember that old song? I was supposed to be at the station and hand you a sandwich when you came rumbling through?"

They regressed. Sandy knew why it was happening. But she left them alone, hoping they could work it out for themselves.

"It was always about Steve," Gretchen mocked. "You're actually doing it right now. You've hijacked this conversation so that it's about you once again. It was such a bad time for Steve. You're like a little baby. Poor little Steve."

Right now, they couldn't work it out on their own.

"You guys are going around in circles," Sandy said. "It's monotonous to listen to."

It got their attention, and not in a good way.

"You know, Sandy, that really doesn't sound like the sort of thing a marriage counselor is supposed to say," Gretchen said. Steamed. She sort of sat up in her chair, straight-backed.

"What is a marriage counselor supposed to say?" Sandy asked.

"That was sarcastic," Gretchen said. "I can't believe you think that's helpful."

"I think your idea of helpful is misguided," Sandy said. "My job isn't to make you feel comfortable."

"Do you want us to be uncomfortable?" Gretchen said. "That can't be the professional thing to do."

"You are already feeling uncomfortable," Sandy said. "I

didn't have anything to do with it. And, by the way, the presumption that you're going to tell me how to conduct these sessions is condescending. I'm not choosing sides here, but Steve isn't actively insulting me."

"Well, you favor Steve, and I'm sick of it," Gretchen lashed out. "I'm really, really tired of his whining and whining, and craving attention. And then getting it! How does he do it? I mean, who cares?"

"When you call someone a vast bottomless emotional pit, you're making a pretty charged statement," Sandy said. "When I heard that, I thought you were saying that Steve demanded so much of you that you didn't have anything left for yourself."

"That's what I was saying," Gretchen said.

"And yet, you had two children and you worked full-time at a job you love and you were successful at that job, so how did you have time for that with Steve demanding everything you had to give?" Sandy said.

"He was incredibly demanding," Gretchen said. "And on top of that, he was having an affair. He was an absolute shit."

Sandy leaned forward and smiled at Gretchen.

"Gretchen, what has got you so riled up today?" Sandy said softly. "What happened?"

"Nothing happened," Gretchen said. "I'm just tired, tired of everything, and really, really tired of you, Steve."

Gretchen looked at Steve and frowned.

"You just keep holding on, holding on, what is the matter with you? What do you want from me?" Gretchen said.

He wants you and you know it, Sandy thought. Obviously. Why are we here?

Steve started to answer, he leaned forward, but before he could say anything, Sandy had her hand up, blocking him, taking the floor. Because he would screw it up.

"What do you think he wants from you?" Sandy said to Gretchen.

"He wants me, he wants my time," Gretchen said.

"How's that?" Sandy said.

"Steve called me twice yesterday," Gretchen said. "He pretended it was about the kids, but then he wants to know if he can see me, he wants to be personal with me, he wants to know who I'm going out with."

"And you don't want to share that stuff with Steve?" Sandy said.

"Of course not," Gretchen said. "And he has no right to know anything about me."

"Rights, rights, I'm so tired of rights," Sandy said.

"Why isn't Steve part of this discussion?" Gretchen said. "Why is it just you and me?"

"I thought the problem was that everything was always about Steve," Sandy said.

"That is the problem," Gretchen said. "It's one of the problems."

"Well, right now, it's all about you and me," Sandy said.

"I said I was tired of what is right. And what is not right. I am. But I'm interested in why you don't want Steve to know anything about your personal life. We need to think about that. But right now, let me ask the converse question. Is there anything about Steve that you want to discuss, other than the general fact that he's such a jerk?"

"No," Gretchen said.

"But you started this whole thing off by mentioning Gabrielle," Sandy said.

"I did not," Gretchen said.

"You said: Gabrielle will discover it soon enough," Sandy said. "Are you having some thoughts about this cooking teacher?"

"No," Gretchen said.

"Okay," Sandy said. "So. You were talking about what a black hole Steve was. Sucking everything in. Isn't that what black holes do?"

Here we go . . .

"By the way, I went on Gabrielle's website, her Italian cooking website," Sandy said. "Did you?" She looked at Gretchen quizzically.

There was a long pause.

"Yes," Gretchen said. "So what?"

"And?" Sandy said.

"What do you want me to say?" Gretchen said defensively. "It's like all *those* websites."

Those?

"It's all so fake," Gretchen said. "That little video of Gabrielle walking in the garden with the guitar music playing. And then she picks a tomato and takes a bite out of it. It's almost soft-core. Come on. Who bites into a tomato?"

Out of the corner of her eye, Sandy saw that Steve had slumped down defensively in his chair.

"And I suppose the fact that she travels to her clients' homes to give them cooking lessons is a bit suspicious," Sandy said.

"You are, like, evil today," Gretchen said in a monotone. "You surprise me."

"Do you think Steve is sleeping with Gabrielle?" Sandy asked.

"I don't care," Gretchen said.

"I'm not sleeping with Gabrielle," Steve said.

"Of course you care," Sandy said to Gretchen. "What got you here in the first place? Why are you separated from Steve? Because he slept with someone."

"No," Gretchen said. "I don't care what Steve does."

"How can you say that?" Sandy said. "You're still going with the rights paradigm? That if you sleep with someone, you can't object to Steve doing it? That isn't true. The simple fact is that it doesn't hurt *you* if *you* sleep with someone. I would guess it barely registers in your deep emotional memory. But Steve, on the other hand? That burns deep into you. You said he was a deep emotional pit. I would guess that translates into the fact that what he does burns deeply into your own emotions. That's how I hear it anyway. Steve takes you into deep emotional and upsetting territory . . . Of course that's scary."

Gretchen was sitting back in her chair, as if she were trying to withdraw from the conversation. Sandy had a vision then: she saw Gretchen sitting back in her chair because there were snakes crawling around on the floor by her feet.

"I am totally lost," Gretchen said.

"I know you are," Sandy said.

Gretchen swung toward Sandy, focused on her.

"I am not lost, I lost track of the conversation," she said, slapping the words down onto the table.

"Which is just what I meant to say," Sandy said.

"No you didn't," Gretchen snapped.

"I did. How would you possibly know what I mean to say?" Sandy said.

"I know," Gretchen said.

"That's pretty much where this started, isn't it," Sandy said. "You were telling me how to do my job. How do you get to tell everyone else what they think, what they mean?"

Sandy leaned forward, she nodded toward Gretchen.

"I know you're thinking that I'm hammering you, that I'm on Steve's side," Sandy said. "Actually, I can't believe Steve was so very stupid for so very long. But it's like Steve had an affair, maybe several affairs, and you pulled out all the ICBMs and you nuked the whole marriage. Okay. Fair enough. A lot of people do that. But then you went to a marriage counselor. That was a bit unusual. Now what do you want? What are you doing here?"

Gretchen rose half out of her chair.

"Are you telling me that it's okay to have an affair? Is that what your advice is?" Gretchen yelled. "Like that's not enough!" She yelled loudly. Sandy watched Steve as the yell pushed him back in his chair even further.

"Will you please sit down," Sandy said.

Gretchen didn't seem to know that she was standing. She looked around, and then, carefully, she sat down.

"Again, when you say, Is it okay to have an affair? you are asking me for a value judgment, and I am very loath to make value judgments. Sometimes it is okay to have an affair," Sandy said. "I guess. I don't know. But what I do think is that it is not okay to not talk to someone. Why can't you just tell Steve what the hell is going on? If you're sleeping with someone, you can't tell him? God, you guys are separated, you are trying to decide what will happen to the most important relationship in your whole life, whether you will get back together or not. This has lifelong implications for your kids. And you can't tell each other what is happening? You will never be able to make decisions sensibly if you can't talk to each other."

Gretchen shook her head, as if she couldn't believe what she was hearing. As if she hadn't heard it. As if when she shook her head, her ears might unlock and she would be able to hear.

"I should tell Steve about who I'm going out with?" she said.

"What do you think?" Sandy said.

"You want me to tell him about sleeping with people?" she said.

"Gretchen," Sandy said slowly, carefully. "I am saying the opposite. What scares you is listening to Steve talk about sleeping with other people. You don't want to listen to what he might tell you on this subject. That is what is going to hurt you. But you turn it around so that it's about yourself. You want to pretend that Steve can't hurt you anymore. He can. He does."

"That is so convoluted," Gretchen said.

"Not really," Sandy said. "It's just painful. And you think it's going to get worse because it's going to happen with Gabrielle."

"I'm not going to debase myself by asking Steve if he's sleeping with Gabrielle," Gretchen said.

"You don't have to because he already told you. He's not," Sandy said.

"And you believed him?" Gretchen yelled. "You actually believed him?"

"Yes," Sandy said. "As a matter of fact I did."

16.

"*Liz is taking* a while to adjust to her day care," Gretchen said. "She can go off on a crying fit that lasts for an hour. It usually happens in the afternoon, which can be a big problem for me if it is on a Monday or a Wednesday.

"Those are the days when I teach my survey course, Introduction to English Literature, with more than a hundred students at the lectures. It's really, really bad to cancel a lecture."

Gretchen hesitated, getting her thoughts together. The issues involving the children were really tough for her, Sandy knew.

"So, if we are going to pick her up on one of those afternoons when I'm teaching, Steve has volunteered to do it, even though it's a week when the kids are my responsibility," Gretchen said.

"If you are going to pick her up?" Sandy said.

"We can let her cry it out for an hour," Gretchen said.

"Have you ever done that?" Sandy asked.

"Not yet," Gretchen said. "Steve has picked her up if I'm teaching. It's only happened twice. I was teaching, they couldn't reach me, so they called Steve and he went and picked Liz up."

"So why is this a problem?" Sandy said, looking at Gretchen.

Gretchen didn't say anything. She looked at Sandy and then looked away.

"Not that you have to have a reason that you can put into words," Sandy said. "If it bothers you, it bothers you."

"It bothers me," Gretchen said. "It's like a feeling that the weather is about to turn. I'm uneasy with it."

"But you can't tell me why?" Sandy said.

Gretchen shook her head. Sandy looked at Steve, who had been too quiet.

"Steve, what do you think might be the reason?" Sandy said.

"Why would you ask Steve about what I'm feeling?" Gretchen said sharply.

"Why not?" Sandy said. "I think it's really good practice to have Steve try to put himself in your shoes. Don't you want him to be able to do that?"

Gretchen gave Sandy a you've-got-to-be-kidding-me look. She didn't roll her eyes, but she might as well have.

Sandy paused, and when Gretchen didn't say anything else, she turned back to Steve.

"What do you think is bothering Gretchen about you taking care of Liz when she has a bad afternoon?" Sandy asked him.

"She's feeling torn," Steve said. "She—"

Sandy interrupted him.

"Steve, tell it to us as if you were Gretchen," Sandy said. "Not she, use I."

Steve looked over at Gretchen, as if he were looking for permission to hijack her feelings.

"Okay," Steve said. "I feel torn between wanting to help my daughter and needing to teach my class."

"So what's wrong with Steve stepping in to help out," Sandy said.

"I don't trust him," Steve said. "I'm not sure why he's being so helpful."

"A hidden agenda?" Sandy said.

"Yes, he always has one," Steve said. "I feel as if he's going to use his kindness against me somehow. But on the other hand, teaching this huge survey course is a big deal. It takes a huge amount of preparation. I have to teach stuff I don't know that well. For example, I'm teaching *Huckleberry Finn*. My expertise is Dickens and Victorian England. The survey course covers five hundred years of literature. It's really hard."

Sandy thought: He knows a lot about Gretchen.

"If it goes well, I might become head of the department," Steve said. "But do I even want that? Do I want more stress that will take me away from the kids? A lot of stuff is up in the air."

"Okay, very nice, Steve. You know all about my career. But the personal stuff is what drives me crazy," Gretchen said, looking at Sandy. "It's like the kids are a line that ties Steve to me and he's pulling me in with them, pulling me closer."

And you resist every inch of the way, Sandy thought.

"I get that is how you feel," Sandy said. "You feel as if Steve is using the kids to get closer to you. But I'm not sure why that is a bad thing?"

"I'm not going to go back to a terrible marriage with a serial adulterer because of the fact that Steve has supposedly changed and now loves his kids," Gretchen said. "I just won't do it. It isn't worth it. And believe me, I've thought about it."

So the fact that you need help two afternoons a week, at the most eight times a month, and then only if everything goes wrong in day care, that equates to going back to a terrible marriage? Sandy wondered.

"Why have you thought about getting back together?" Sandy asked.

"I've thought about getting back together with Steve because of the kids," Gretchen said. "Obviously. Everyone in this situation thinks that."

Actually, they don't, Sandy thought. Some think about murder. Or running away with the kids to a foreign country.

"And going back with Steve just because of the kids would be a bad thing?" Sandy said.

"You can't be serious," Gretchen said. "Are you trying to provoke me? Is that a tool of modern marriage counseling?"

"Oh, I'm completely serious," Sandy said. "Why would that be a bad thing?"

She saw Steve looking hard at Gretchen.

"It isn't even worth discussing," Gretchen said.

"Gretchen, I'm curious about something," Sandy said. She leaned forward, in a friendly sort of way, as if she wanted to talk to Gretchen like they were girlfriends. "Do you and Steve talk on the telephone?"

"Of course we talk on the telephone," Gretchen said, sounding to Sandy a bit as if she were talking to a friend who was a little slow, Sandy expecting Gretchen to add something like *What do you expect?*

"So how often?" Sandy said.

"These days, a couple of times a week," Gretchen said.

"I think you talk more than a couple of times a week," Sandy said. "I think you talk almost every day."

"I don't get the point of this," Gretchen said.

"The point of it is, you are enmeshed with Steve," Sandy said.

"I talk to Steve to see how the kids are, to make sure we haven't forgotten stuff," Gretchen said.

"I'm not trying to be a bad guy here, Gretchen," Sandy said. "I'm not trying to beat you over the head with this—"

"It sort of feels that way," Gretchen said, interrupting. "Did Steve tell you that we talked on the phone every day?"

"No, actually, I came to that conclusion myself," Sandy said, bemused. Like this was hard to figure out?

"Okay, so what?" Gretchen said. "I admit that I've been enmeshed with Steve in the past. It was a huge problem. But I'm trying to cut the ties."

Not exactly, Sandy thought. You've got yourself a safe distance from Steve, a safe distance, and now that you feel safe, you're probing to see what there is between you. Sandy wanted to shake Gretchen, stare her in the eyes, ask: What do you think about Steve right now, this instant?

"Do you think Steve is tapping your phone, reading your e-mails, that he has bugs in your apartment?" Sandy asked.

"Of course not," Gretchen said. "At least I don't think so," she added.

"So how does he know what you're teaching? How much

time you have to spend preparing to teach? How does he know that there is a chance you might become head of the department? How does he know you're teaching *Huckleberry Finn*?" Sandy said.

Sandy leaned even more in Gretchen's direction, and said in a soft voice: "Because you tell him, Gretchen. On those phone calls, the ones you don't think are going on. And that's okay."

"That's crazy," Gretchen said.

"Is that the second time you've said I'm crazy?" Sandy said. "The second time today?"

"I didn't mean it that way," Gretchen said. "It's just like you're pushing me, and I don't like to be pushed."

"I know," Sandy said. She smiled at Gretchen. "Despite that, would you play along with me?"

"It depends on the game," Gretchen said.

"Six months ago, Gretchen, you were setting limits on Steve. He'd call you and you wouldn't answer. You had Steve text you to find out when he could call you. Remember?" Sandy said.

"I remember," Gretchen said.

"But you're not doing that anymore, are you?" Sandy said.

"No," Gretchen said. "I'm not."

"So what's happening?" Sandy said.

"It's easier to talk to Steve," Gretchen said. "There's no doubt about it. He is just easier. I admit that."

"Do you ever call him?" Sandy asked.

"Yes," Gretchen said. "I admit that."

"Do you ever call him just to talk?" Sandy asked.

"Not really," Gretchen said. "I think there's always a reason."

"Like you just want to talk?" Sandy said. "That would be a reason, right?"

Gretchen looked away, and Sandy saw that she was twirling a piece of her blond hair that had fallen forward over her shoulder.

"Did you talk to Steve last night?" Sandy asked.

"Yes I did," Gretchen said. She looked at Steve, then back to Sandy.

"So how did it happen that you talked with Steve last night?" Sandy said.

"I called him," Gretchen said. She shook her head. "I see where this is going. You think because I talk to Steve, something is happening between us, we're getting closer. Right?"

"Not quite," Sandy said. "I think both of you are more secure. Both of you know that you can live on your own. I think it's like you both are exploring the relationship that exists between you now. It's a new relationship. So I'm curious about what you talk about and how you talk when you talk on the phone. So why don't you do that now?"

"How is this supposed to work?" Steve said.

"Let's just say it's last night, and Gretchen calls you on the phone," Sandy said. She looked at Gretchen.

"Why is this a good idea?" Gretchen said.

"Imagine that we're going to spread your relationship out on the floor and look it over, just as if it were Penelope's weaving," Sandy said.

"If it's Penelope's weaving, then we take it apart at night and weave it back again the next day," Gretchen said.

"The trick is to know the pattern," Sandy said. "Call Steve."

Gretchen thought it over, and then she pointed her finger at Steve.

"You go," she said.

"Hello," Steve said, imagining that Gretchen had called him.

"Can you talk?" Gretchen said.

"The kids are in bed, it's quiet, I can talk," Steve said.

"So Gabrielle isn't there?" Gretchen said.

"No, Gabrielle isn't here," Steve said. "I'm all by myself. If the kids are here, I'm always by myself. So I'm available if you want to come over and keep me company."

"Unfortunately, I'm in my own bed and warm as toast, so I'm not coming over, for lots of good reasons," Gretchen said.

"That's too bad," Steve said. "So how are you doing? What's up?"

Gretchen raised her hand.

"No, at this point, I believe you said something like, How come that moronic drama professor isn't in bed with you?" Gretchen said.

"Maybe I said, How are things going with the drama teacher?" Steve said.

"So how are things going with the drama professor?" Sandy said.

Gretchen looked at Sandy and then back to Steve.

"You know, Steve, I really called to find out how it went with the kids today. How did Liz do at preschool?" Gretchen said.

"She did better," Steve said. "I stayed for the first half hour and then she said, It's okay, Daddy, you can go. And it was hard to leave when she said that. It was like she was trying to be so strong. She hates that place."

"We have to fix this," Gretchen said.

"In six months, she can go to Pacific Primary," Steve said. "It's a better school and she'll like that she's there with Chris."

"Yes, that will help," Gretchen said. "I better hang up. I'm tired. It's late."

"You, you, I miss you," Steve said. He was emotional. He had suddenly transitioned right into the phone call. It was real. For Steve, it was happening.

"I know you do," Gretchen said.

"So you're just sitting there?" Steve said. "Really. Why don't you come over?"

"It wouldn't be a good thing. I'm not ready for that," Gretchen said.

"When are you going to be ready?" Steve said.

"If you are going to mess with me, I'm hanging up,"

Gretchen said. She looked over at Sandy, who read her look as if this were getting too real.

"I'm sorry," Steve said.

"You said you were sorry?" Sandy said to Steve. She looked at Gretchen.

"Yes, he did," Gretchen said.

"I was sorry," Steve said.

You guys are better, Sandy thought, much better. That didn't mean they would necessarily get back together, but they were definitely weaving something new.

17.

"I'm confused about what went on last weekend," Gretchen said. "Apparently you took the kids on a huge hike in the hills that lasted all day? And you met up with Gabrielle?"

"No," Steve said. "What happened is, I took the kids on a walk in Golden Gate Park, but we walked the entire way to the ocean, and then back again, more than six miles. We had lunch at the Beach Chalet. So to them it felt like a huge hike, but we never left the city. It was an urban adventure. I was proud of them. It was a long walk, but they didn't complain, although I had to put Liz on my shoulders the last mile.

"As for Gabrielle, she wasn't on the hike. She was running in the park, which she does every day, and she saw us and stopped to say hello. I introduced her to the kids. They had never met her before."

"Gabrielle had never met the kids?" Gretchen said.

"Nope," Steve said.

"Why don't you include her?" Gretchen asked.

"Why would I do that?" Steve said. "I don't want them to get the wrong idea."

"What wrong idea?" Gretchen said.

Steve looked uncomfortable. He shrugged.

"You know, like I have a girlfriend," Steve said.

"Do you have a girlfriend?" Gretchen asked.

"Am I going out with Gabrielle?" Steve said. "Yes, I've gone out with Gabrielle, but I wouldn't call her a girlfriend. She's a friend."

"It's a little more than that, isn't it?" Gretchen said.

"I'm not asking you about who you're going out with," Steve said.

"Ask anything you want," Gretchen said. "I still talk to Bill, but I haven't seen him in a while, as you know, it's a complicated relationship. As I told you, I went out with a colleague a couple of times. He teaches in the drama department?

Would you like to know anything about that? I slept with him."

Sandy could see several thoughts flash in Steve's face, just below the surface. But he took a second to think it over and then let them all sink down into the fiery pit at the back of his brain where his bad thoughts screamed and twisted and tried to climb out.

"You, on the other hand, don't seem to want to talk about Gabrielle," Gretchen said. "How many times have you been away for the weekend with her?"

"I haven't been away for the weekend with her and I don't see what this is about," Steve said. "Why do we have to define my relationship with Gabrielle? What does it matter?"

Gretchen leaned forward.

"Don't you think it matters to Gabrielle?" Gretchen said.

"I have no idea," Steve said.

Sandy saw that Gretchen was shoveling coal into the boiler of this locomotive, and it was slowly picking up steam. Once it got going, it was going to be hard to stop.

"Don't you think she deserves to know how you think about her? What you think about the relationship?" Gretchen said evenly.

"Sandy has made me highly suspect about what people deserve," Steve said. "But Gabrielle certainly expects me to be honest with her, and I'm trying to be."

"Steve," Gretchen said, as if his attention was wandering and she needed to call him back, refocus him. "Steve," she said again. "Gabrielle is the only woman you're seeing, isn't she? She's aware of that, right? That must mean something to her."

"She's not the only woman I'm seeing," Steve said.

"You're kidding," Gretchen said in a singed, angry voice. "You are two-timing Gabrielle?"

Gretchen shook her finger at Steve.

"You're a real piece of work, aren't you?" Gretchen said.

"You're the other woman I'm seeing," Steve said. "I see you here, with Sandy once a week, and we see each other at least four or five other times during the week, and we also talk on the phone. I think it's important that Gabrielle knows that. She needs to know that I'm still invested in you."

Sandy thought that might back Gretchen off, that it might throw a switch and send the train down another track, but it didn't. The runaway train just gathered speed.

"Very smart," Gretchen said. "But it's exactly the same thing as it would be if you were going out with another woman. You're leading Gabrielle on, you're letting her believe that you're going to be there long-term."

It was all misdirection, but could Steve see it? If Gretchen was ever going to get back together with Steve, if she was ever going to be happy whether she was with Steve or not, she needed to understand what she was doing. And so did Steve.

"Gretchen, when I met Gabby, she was just breaking up with a guy she'd been with for three years. She doesn't want a serious new relationship. I'm safe because I'm still wrapped up with you, whether you're wrapped up with me or not. I'm safe for Gabby," Steve said.

"You actually believe that?" Gretchen said. "You can't see what's right in front of your face?"

Steve turned his hands palms up—the expression saying, Are you crazy? He shook his head.

"Is Gabrielle going out with anyone else?" Gretchen said.

"I don't think so," Steve said.

"You'd be angry if she was, wouldn't you?" Gretchen snapped.

Steve shut his eyes. He took several deep breaths, getting centered. Then he opened his eyes and stared at Gretchen.

"I don't get it," Steve said. "And I resent it. I've answered the questions, I've told you everything, and you still keep hammering away."

"Why do you resent it?" Sandy said. It was the first time she'd spoken since the beginning of this session. She had been racing along with them, and now she'd jumped into the cab of the locomotive; she was going to take this runaway train down another track.

"I mean, what am I supposed to do about Gabrielle? I'm honest with her. Gabrielle is a big girl. She can take care of herself," Steve said.

"You said you resent Gretchen hammering away at you over Gabrielle," Sandy said. "Didn't you?"

"Yes," Steve said.

"Okay, well, why do you resent it?" Sandy said.

"It's gratuitous," Steve said.

"Is it? I'm not so sure," Sandy said.

Sandy looked at Gretchen. Let's back this train up, Sandy thought, and she threw the train into reverse.

"Gretchen, this all started out because your children told you they went on a mystical hike with Steve, a daylong hike where they encountered all sorts of wonderful things, including meeting a beautiful dark-haired Italian princess," Sandy said. "Or something like that.

"But it turns out that it was a hike right here in the city, and Gabrielle was just a jogger who happened by."

Sandy folded her hands in her lap. She thought, It is amazing, isn't it, how brilliantly Gretchen uses misdirection so that she gets what she wants but never reveals her feelings.

"Isn't that pretty much how this all started?" Sandy said, looking at Gretchen, who said nothing.

"Then we went down this path, which started with you accusing Steve of not caring about Gabrielle's feelings." Sandy said. "Right?"

Gretchen said nothing.

"Come on," Sandy said to Gretchen. "You don't want to live this way. It makes life so confusing, no one can figure out what's up."

"I don't get it," Gretchen said slowly.

"That was Steve's line," Sandy said. "You've managed to completely confuse him. But I don't think you're confused."

"But I am," Gretchen said.

"Do you actually care about Gabrielle's feelings?" Sandy said.

"Yes I do," Gretchen said. "At least I think Steve needs to be aware that she has feelings and respect that."

Come on, Gretchen, Sandy thought.

"Do you want Steve to fall in love with Gabrielle?" Sandy asked Gretchen.

"That's Steve's business," Gretchen said quietly.

Oh, please, Sandy thought. She had backed the train past the switch in the track, and now she threw the switch and pushed the train forward down the new direction.

"That's not an answer," Sandy said.

"All right," Gretchen said innocently. "No, I don't want Steve and Gabrielle to fall in love. I want Steve to spend the rest of his days alone, lonely and miserable and unloved."

"But we both know that isn't going to happen," Sandy said gently.

"I suppose not," Gretchen said. "Unfortunately."

And it's not going to happen to you either, Sandy thought, though you're worried about it.

"Are you ready to give Steve up?" Sandy said.

"Not exactly," Gretchen said.

"I'll take that as a no," Sandy said. "All of this discussion has been to make sure that he's still here. But you couldn't say that. Not directly. You need to learn to say what you mean. Steve? I don't think he's going to learn to translate anytime soon. Well, he will, hopefully, at some point. But for now, it's up to you."

She saw that Gretchen's eyes were wet. It was tough for her. Sandy understood that. Gretchen was full of pride.

"I'm coming here every week," Gretchen said. "I never miss a session. I think that gives me some rights."

Not rights again, Sandy thought, but she knew that what Gretchen meant was that she had expectations that arose out of these sessions.

"So you come here in good faith every week," Sandy said. "And what does that lead you to expect?"

Now Gretchen looked hard at Steve.

"You're going to get the wrong idea, I know it," Gretchen said. "It's not like I love you or want to spend the rest of my life with you."

Tears had formed in the corners of her eyes.

"Do you get that?" Gretchen said. "It's only that I feel as if I have an option on you, an option that I can exercise at my discretion. An option that expires *when I say it expires*."

Steve had an investment. Gretchen had an option. They had so much to learn about how to speak about love, Sandy thought. But they were trying.

Sandy handed Gretchen the box of tissues.

"Can I see you alone?" Gretchen asked Sandy.

18.

"*This conversation is* just between us?" Gretchen asked.

She paused, looking at Sandy.

"Everything is just between us," Sandy said. "But at some point, anything you tell me in private goes to Steve if he needs to hear it. He doesn't need to hear everything, but I decide what he needs to know."

"I really don't want Steve to know about this," Gretchen said.

"Then you shouldn't tell me," Sandy said. "Or." She smiled at Gretchen. "Or, you could trust me."

"I don't trust you," Gretchen said.

Sandy laughed, couldn't help herself, appreciating Gretchen's honesty.

"Why don't you trust me?" Sandy asked.

"I don't feel as if you are on my side," Gretchen said.

"No, I'm not on your side," Sandy said.

"There's something here I'm not seeing," Gretchen said. She looked around the room, as if there were something in it she was missing. Her eyes stopped on the green chair, the one that didn't match, the one that no one sat in. Then her eyes moved on.

Who's sitting in the chair, Gretchen? Sandy thought. Make the leap.

"You're feeling something going on beneath the surface," Sandy said. "That feeling is my point of view. You could call it a side. If you like, you could say I side with the marriage. At the very least I try to speak for the marriage. That's what you're feeling."

An idea flicked across Gretchen's face.

"I get it," Gretchen said. "That's why it feels like you're on Steve's side. He wants to revivify the marriage too."

It was nice for Sandy to work with someone who used a word like *revivify*. But smart as she was, Gretchen didn't get it.

"No, that's not quite right," Sandy said. "I try to speak

for the marriage because neither of you is. This isn't a marriage where someone is beating the other one up. Or where someone is gambling away everything the family owns, or someone can't hold a job because they're drunk or high. As a matter of fact, this is a marriage that, in material terms, has been very successful. Steve made money, you got tenure, you have two smart, terrific children. You put something together here, and it took effort. Work. You built a marriage. That's the side I'm on, that's who I speak for, because neither of you does. The invisible thing you built. It's something."

"Look: that is so hippy-dippy, so happy-go-lucky, so you, Sandy," Gretchen said. "Steve lied to me, he cheated on me. He did it repeatedly. He didn't support my work. We were two independent contractors who made a strategic alliance. I just didn't realize that was all we had."

"As opposed to what? True love?" Sandy asked.

"Something like that," Gretchen said. "I'm not embarrassed to say it. True love."

"Look," Sandy said. She leaned back in her chair and turned a bit away from Gretchen. Then Sandy sort of shrugged. "I know that you have something to tell me. I sense we're off on a bit of a tangent. My hunch is that what you want to talk about has something to do with Gabrielle. But let's take this tangent a bit further, and wait on discussing Gabrielle. Okay?"

Gretchen nodded.

"I really admire the fact that you were not willing to

accept a marriage where your husband was having affairs. That's not a good marriage. It's so careless, so unfeeling. It's insufferable. Adultery is just a killer, it hurts so much. I know about it, actually. Sometime I'll tell you that story.

"You were absolutely right to throw Steve out of the house, and to separate. You wanted more than that kind of life. I applaud you for it. But there's a reason we're here in my office, isn't there? And you're not sitting in a lawyer's office."

"Yes," Gretchen said. "I'm a fucking idiot."

"I don't think so," Sandy said.

"I am. I think he can change," Gretchen said.

He has changed, Sandy thought, and you pushed him to it. Sandy handed her the box of tissues and Gretchen pulled one out and dabbed her eyes.

"It's just a killer, isn't it," Sandy said. "I mean, the fact that he slept with someone else."

"It is," Gretchen said, almost lightly. "I could never trust him again."

"Two completely different issues," Sandy said. "I mean the pain he caused you and whether you can trust him."

Gretchen nodded slowly.

"Yes they are, aren't they?" Gretchen said softly, thinking.

"So the pain is one thing," Sandy said. "Let's not deal with that now. Let's talk about the trust."

"It's all gone," Gretchen said. It just flowed out of her spontaneously, a huge hurt, a purge.

This is what she came to talk to me about, Sandy realized. Not Gabrielle. Or maybe they're related?

"What about the trust?" Sandy said, and watched Gretchen gather herself together. It takes so much out of her to talk about her feelings. Sandy can feel the difficulty, see it.

Suddenly, Sandy saw Gretchen flick into the moment, into right now, her feelings available to her without mediation.

"I had an insane idea that Steve had Gabrielle over at his place when he had the kids," Gretchen said after a moment. "It was a nightmare. I woke up at three in the morning, sure she was there. I was sweaty, crazy. I just can't tell you how real this dream was."

Sandy wished that Steve could hear Gretchen. If he could, he would understand why Gretchen had slept with other men, using them to drive away the night.

"I tried to get back to sleep and I couldn't. I mean, I have so much work piled up, but all I could think about was Steve with Gabrielle in his bed and the kids just down the hall. What if they woke up? What if they went to Steve's room?"

Gretchen paused, crossed her arms, leaned back in the chair, looked out the window, got herself together. Sandy watched and waited, thinking Gretchen was so far ahead of the game. Sandy was sure Steve wasn't sleeping with Gabrielle, not yet. And here was Gretchen, already dealing with it as a reality.

"I drove over to Steve's house at five in the morning," Gretchen said. "I sat there in my car for three hours. I waited until Steve came out with the kids, put them in the car, and took them to school."

"Just Steve, I take it," Sandy said.

"No one with him. I watched the door after he left to see if anyone else came out," Gretchen said. "I'm crazy, right? I'm telling you, I'm a wreck. What's happening to me?"

Good question. You went over to Steve's house at five in the morning. You sat outside his house for three hours. Was it all for fear of Gabrielle and the kids in the next room?

That was part of it, but you also wanted Steve, Sandy thought. You moved toward him like a sleepwalker, unconsciously. You approached his doorstep.

And there you stopped. You couldn't go in. Sandy thought of the last scene in *The Searchers*: John Wayne at the doorstep of the family home. The family is finally happily reunited inside. Wayne is still on the porch. And the door closes, shutting him out.

Gretchen was scared that the door would close on her.

"This is hard stuff," Sandy said. Gretchen was tearing up again and Sandy handed her the tissue box.

"I don't want a blended family," Gretchen said. "I hate the term *blended family*, like we're a blended whiskey."

This was honest. Good for Gretchen. So what can you do about not having one? Sometimes there aren't many other choices. But you still have them, Gretchen. Gretchen handed Sandy back the tissues.

"I need more out of life. I can't move forward. I'm stuck," Gretchen said. "Miserable."

"You look really tired," Sandy said.

"You mean I look like shit," Gretchen said.

No, Gretchen was still beautiful, but different. She'd acquired a sort of patina, beauty tempered by suffering.

"You just look tired," Sandy said, realizing she'd had this conversation with Gretchen before, Gretchen attacking the same demons again.

"I forget stuff, I'm unsure, tentative when I'm teaching. I'm really unhappy," Gretchen said.

"I'm sorry," Sandy said.

"Remember that drama professor from a month ago?" Gretchen said. "He still won't leave me alone. What's wrong with him?"

"So tell him you don't like him, tell him to get lost," Sandy said.

"What?" Gretchen said. "How could I tell him that?"

"You sound trapped," Sandy said. "But you're springing the trap yourself. What is it? Good manners? You don't want to hurt anyone's feelings? This has got to stop, Gretchen. No more pleasing people. If you ever want to have a real marriage you have to stop pleasing people. Tell the drama guy to get out of your life. Immediately. Go. Gone."

"I don't know," Gretchen said softly. Sandy could see the tumblers of her brain spinning, recalculating.

"I was in love with Steve," Gretchen said, her mind jumping, explaining to herself why Steve was different.

"I know you were," Sandy said, thinking, You are in love with Steve.

"I can't live with Steve again," Gretchen said.

"But you hate blended families and you married Steve because you loved him," Sandy said.

Gretchen's blue eyes narrowed.

"Why does Steve always get what he wants?" Gretchen said angrily.

"I'd say he's had a hell of a time the past months. A real killer," Sandy said. "He's been slammed and knocked down. And somehow he's managed to get back on his feet again and again."

"So what!" Gretchen said loudly. "I mean, poor Steve."

Sandy let Gretchen's anger lie there between them.

"My mother is coming out here to see me and the kids," Gretchen said after a few moments. "She asked me if I would mind if she had lunch with Steve. It's like women—they all want to help Steve out. He has his cleaning woman, he has his beautiful Italian cook, he has his own mother, who would do anything for him. And now he has my mother too. I mean, why? Why?"

Sandy wanted to swing the conversation back to where they'd started, to the problem Gretchen couldn't solve.

"Yes, it feels unfair. But can we go back to the issue of you going over to Steve's in the middle of the night?" Sandy said.

Gretchen didn't want to, Sandy read it in her movement as she pushed back in her seat.

"You were worried about Gabrielle," Sandy said.

"I don't know," Gretchen said stubbornly. "I don't care."

"Oh yes you do," Sandy said. "Come on. We've been through this before. Don't you realize that we've talked about this, in almost these exact words?"

Gretchen looked off toward the corner of the room.

"I know we talked about this before," Gretchen said. "I'm sorry."

"Don't be. Let me ask you something else. If Steve tells you that he wants to talk to you about Gabrielle, what are you going to do?" Sandy said.

"I guess I'll listen," Gretchen said.

"Yes, you should do that," Sandy said.

Gretchen looked off again.

"Getting back together with Steve," Gretchen said slowly. "At some point, if I don't get back together with Steve, he will find someone else. I know it."

"At some point, yes, someone, or Gabrielle in particular, could be a real issue," Sandy said. "But right now, you could just tell Steve that you really didn't want him to see Gabrielle, and he'd do it."

Gretchen nodded. She was thinking.

"Maybe," Gretchen said. "I'm not going to do that. But I'd like to know if we are close to the point of no return."

Everyone had a button. Steve had one to make Bill disappear. Gretchen had one she could use on Gabrielle. And Sandy had one now. She could press it and get them back together. She could say to Gretchen, You need to get back with Steve now, or he'll find someone else.

"Are we close to that point of no return?" Gretchen asked. "Please. Tell me, Sandy."

"I don't think so," Sandy said.

What if I'm wrong, Sandy thought. What if I don't press the button and Steve goes off with Gabrielle? What if I've misjudged the whole situation?

"Will you tell me if we get close to it?" Gretchen asked.

"You tell me," Sandy said. "You know Steve better than I do. You'll know if you get close to that point."

"Will I?"

"I promise you," Sandy said. What are you promising? Sandy wondered. What can you really deliver?

"Steve and I are separated," Gretchen said. "But I want to treat him as if he was still my husband, as if we were still married."

As if you still trusted each other, Sandy thought. That's what Gretchen meant.

"Are you divorced? No. Not only can you treat him as your husband, he is your husband," Sandy said.

"Do you want us to get back together?" Gretchen asked suddenly.

"That's not my call," Sandy said.

What a cop-out, Sandy thought, sort of ashamed of herself. Yes, Gretchen, yes, I want you to get back together, but you have to do it yourself.

"I'm really, really angry with Steve," Gretchen said.

I know that, you went over to his house at five in the morning, you waited in your car for three hours. I see your anger, Sandy thought.

"I think your anger is something you need to talk to Steve about," Sandy said.

"I don't want to be intimate with you," Gretchen said fiercely, loudly. She sat straight in her chair. "I don't want to get back together with you."

"With Steve," Sandy said.

"Yes, I'm a wreck, I mean, I won't get back together with Steve," Gretchen said.

"Except you hate blended families, and you hide in your car outside Steve's house for hours in the middle of the night, you've slept with people you don't like," Sandy said. "And yet you don't believe you can talk about any of this with Steve. Come on. Give me a break."

"I went to his house because he's fucking someone when he's got the kids," Gretchen howled.

"But he wasn't," Sandy said.

"But he could have been," Gretchen screamed.

19.

"*But he could have been,*" Gretchen screamed. And slumped back in her chair, exhausted.

They sat in the office quietly. It felt to Sandy as if they had crossed through some barrier, emerged on the other side. This was a new session now.

"While you were sitting in the car outside Steve's house?" Sandy said. "Why didn't you ring the doorbell?"

"At four in the morning, when the kids were asleep?" Gretchen said.

"You said you went over at five and stayed in your car for three hours. So you were there at seven when the kids were waking up and Steve would probably have loved to have some help with them," Sandy said.

"What if Gabrielle had been there?" Gretchen said.

"What if she was?"

"What would I have done?"

"You weren't carrying a gun or a knife. You would have introduced yourself," Sandy said. "And you would have had some answers. But Gabrielle wasn't going to be there. So you would have rung the bell, walked in, and said to Steve, I missed the kids."

Gretchen nodded. She saw something. Sandy read it in her face.

"I could have called him on my cell phone and then walked in," Gretchen said.

"You could have said you happened to be in the neighborhood," Sandy added.

"Come on," Gretchen said. But she grinned. "So, you said you were on the side of the marriage. What exactly does that mean? Do you mean you favor marriage as a social good?"

"Oh no," Sandy said. "I have no idea about that. I'm talking specifically about your marriage. The particular idiosyncratic marriage that you and Steve put together."

Sandy looked around the room, then back at Gretchen.

"I see the marriage as independent of either of you. You guys built this entity, this marriage. You put a lot of work into it. Houses, children. I speak for this entity you created. Because neither of you is going to."

"Steve trashed our marriage," Gretchen said.

And yet you're here, Sandy thought.

"Yes, he did, but the marriage is still here," Sandy said. "Can you sense it?"

Gretchen looked at Sandy with a look that implied: This marriage counselor is crazy.

"Don't you feel it?" Sandy asked.

"No, actually I don't," Gretchen said. "I guess I've just been hurt too much."

You don't feel it? Sandy thought. You feel it so much you were ready to divorce Steve. The marriage is so powerful that you want to kill Steve for hurting it. You have been hurt so much because the marriage was so important.

"Can I ask something that is probably really dumb?" Gretchen said.

"There is no dumb," Sandy said. "Ask me anything."

"There are three Scandinavian armchairs in here. But there is a fourth chair," Gretchen said. "And it's sort of a Victorian chair covered in green linen. An old-fashioned chair. Why this fourth chair?"

"You're on a roll," Sandy said. "You tell me."

"Well, the couple wouldn't sit in that chair. So, if I follow your logic, that chair, the green one, is the chair for the marriage," Gretchen said. Her eyes opened wide. She stared at Sandy. Who was this woman? "But that's crazy. That couldn't possibly be true, could it?"

"Yes, I keep that chair in the office to remind me that I speak for the marriage. That is the marriage's chair," Sandy said. "You see, the marriage can't speak for itself."

Gretchen stared at the green chair, as if there were something, someone, sitting in it.

Then Gretchen looked away from the chair, at the window and then back at Sandy.

"Sandy, you are sounding delusional," Gretchen said.

"Am I?" Sandy said. "Next time, when you and Steve are sitting here together with me, see if you can feel your marriage sitting here with us. Just humor me and try. Okay?"

"I don't even know how I would do that," Gretchen said.

"Look at the chair. Try to see the marriage, feel how it's feeling, even how it's looking," Sandy said. "It may sound crazy, but you need some new ideas. The old ones didn't work that well, did they?"

Gretchen was looking back at the green chair.

"No," Gretchen said slowly. "No, they didn't."

"So try something new, something you think is delusional," Sandy said. "Have a conversation with your marriage."

"You said it doesn't talk," Gretchen said.

"Not out loud," Sandy said. "But if you listen closely enough, you'll hear it."

"You're going to tell me what my nonexistent marriage

is saying from a chair it isn't in?" Gretchen said. And yet, despite this cynical remark, she was, in fact, smiling.

Sandy smiled in return.

"Not quite, Gretchen. I'm not going to tell you what your marriage is saying," Sandy said. "You're going to tell me what your marriage is saying. I'm just going to teach you to listen to it."

20.

"There is a black Mercedes AMG C63 sitting in your parking lot, Sandy," Steve said when they were all seated.

"Yes, there is," Sandy said. "It's mine."

"You're kidding me," Steve said.

"I can't have a nice car?" Sandy said.

"You traded in your Prius?"

"I got the Mercedes from my mother," Sandy said. "I'll have a plaque made, like the one on the building. Actually I may get rid of it. We'll see. Hey, it's kind of fun, but I wouldn't be driving it, except my Prius is getting its checkup. Do you miss your Mercedes?"

"No," Steve said. "When I saw yours, I thought it was mine, come back to haunt me, like a demon from the underworld."

"I can relate to that," Sandy said. "Gretchen, I lived with my dad during high school. Steve knows about it. My mom would stalk me in her C63. I would hear the booming engine and run for it, a demon chasing me all over the city."

"When I saw the car, I thought Steve had relapsed, but then I saw his Subaru," Gretchen said.

"Have you relapsed, Steve?" Sandy asked. "I want you to look at Gretchen and tell me what you see."

"Like what we did before?" Steve asked. Sandy nodded.

Steve looked at Gretchen, and she looked back at him. He looked off and then back at her.

"Okay, I see a woman in her mid-thirties, very beautiful, blond hair, blue eyes, she is dressed professionally, has almost no jewelry on, just small gold circle earrings, a white blouse, a dark blue fitted skirt, and black low shoes, flats," Steve said. "All in all, as I said, she looks competent, in control."

"Let's take this a little further," Sandy said. "Why don't you just look at Gretchen for a couple of minutes."

"I'm not sure I like being objectified," Gretchen said. "More simply, I don't think I like being stared at."

"I invite you to stare at Steve while he stares at you," Sandy said. "I'm going to ask you about Steve."

Gretchen shrugged. It was noncommittal. She wasn't necessarily buying into this exercise. But she looked at Steve and went along with it.

A few minutes went by.

"Okay, I'm trying to look deeper," Steve said. "So Gretchen is wearing a white blouse with no jewelry. But that white blouse, I happen to know, came from Paris, because Gretchen bought it there. And when you look at it, it has a high collar that is kind of . . ."

He paused, still looking at Gretchen, trying to find the right words.

"So, it's got a bit of France when they had musketeers and big boots, and wore swords. It's really simple, but the sleeves have four buttons on the cuffs, and the collar is definitely romantic," Steve said. "And I happen to know, though I can't see it from here, that there is a double seam in the back."

"Go on," Sandy said. "More."

"I happen to know that Gretchen's hair, sort of palomino colored, is natural, and when I look at it, it seems romantic too, like it's gold, but gold in layers, it's really beautiful," Steve said. "You know, it's romantic too, because it's long hair, it sweeps down over her shoulders, it's long and thick."

"Take it another step, will you?" Sandy said, half expecting Gretchen to object, but Gretchen didn't. She sat there quietly, her beautiful romantic blue eyes focused on Steve.

"Okay, the simple blue skirt isn't so simple either, it's a dark, almost black, blue and it contrasts with the white blouse, and it's not form-fitting, hugging, but it's sexy too, it doesn't hide her body," Steve said.

Again, Sandy thought that might bring out Gretchen's anger, but she sat there, looking at Steve. Waiting her turn?

"Okay, I notice the fact that Gretchen has kicked off one of her shoes, and that foot is resting over the one that still has a shoe on," Steve said. "And I never noticed this before, but I can see the heel of the shoe that Gretchen has kicked off has a sort of copper half circle around the back of it, just on top of the low heel, it's like a spur."

"That's pretty good," Sandy said. "How are you feeling right now?"

She was pretty sure what he was feeling and she wanted it on the table. How could she know his feelings? It came from Steve to her in a hundred small ways, from his eyes, to his hands gripping his chair, to the arch of his backbone.

"I'm feeling sad," Steve said. "And I'm feeling incredibly stupid, which is nothing new, it's been a recurring theme in these sessions."

"Why are you sad right now?" Sandy asked.

"Well," Steve said. "Okay, looking at Gretchen for so long, I'm sort of turned on."

"This is crazy," Gretchen said loudly. "This is supposed to be serious?"

"It is serious," Sandy said. "And I think you know it. It's very serious." She looked at Steve.

"Why are you feeling aroused?" Sandy asked Steve.

"Gretchen is like some beautiful woman who rides a horse to meet her lover, the highwayman," Steve said.

"Come on," Gretchen said.

"And?" Sandy asked.

"The highwayman betrays her," Steve said.

"And?" Sandy asked.

"She pulls out the silver inlaid dueling pistols from the finely tooled leather holsters lashed to the pommel of the saddle of her big black horse and shoots the highwayman dead," Steve said.

"This is so melodramatic," Gretchen said. "I am not some character in a Brontë novel. Or in the Alfred Noyes poem. And I'm not Anita Garibaldi, on a big galloping black horse, with a pistol in one hand and a baby in the other. And this is not marriage counseling. And I've done research."

Sandy sat up straight, she blinked. Okay, Gretchen, take it away.

"And what did you find in your research?" Sandy said.

"I mean, what theory of marriage counseling is this?" Gretchen said. "Are you doing Structural Family Therapy? Milan Family Therapy? Solution Focused Therapy? Narrative Therapy? No. This is like a freshman enrichment seminar in college."

"Like the one where you met Steve?" Sandy asked.

"Yes, like Elizabeth and Her Poetry, where I met Steve," Gretchen said.

"That was the one where he had an insight about Queen Elizabeth's dress?" Sandy asked.

"Which is all he's doing now," Gretchen said in frustration.

"Which is when you fell in love with him," Sandy said.

"You ask us to look at each other and describe each other," Gretchen said hard, demanding. "But what we look like, particularly what Steve looks like, can change all the time. I look at Steve now, and he's rugged, cords or jeans, flannel shirts, I mean, he used to get his shirts handmade, now he doesn't even get them pressed. He's all outdoorsy and friendly. What I'm saying is that someone like Steve changes his look at will, to suit his purposes."

"Maybe he's just changed," Sandy said. "Why don't you look at him?"

"I just described him," Gretchen said.

"Come on, Gretchen," Sandy said.

"No! Can we back up for a second," Gretchen said. "Steve looked at me and saw a romantic. He felt badly because he had betrayed the romantic part of me. Okay, it's true that I do have an inclination to dress as a sort of austere romantic. And I would like to believe that whoever I'm with really loves me. But I think Steve missed the austere side.

"You see, we have two children. We both had careers. We had a sort of team going. And, as a matter of fact, we did have uniforms. Steve was the protective businessman who was going to make sure the team was provided for. I was the loving supermom who was able to take most of the kid responsibility while also having my own career, though not a career with as much pizzazz as that of my super Silicon Valley husband.

"Even the kids knew they were part of the team, that they were supposed to do well, like that was just required, they had to pull their weight and they did.

"So then, Steve doesn't just betray me, he betrays the whole team, the whole project, everything we've been working to build. It wasn't romantic love. It was making sure the kids' lunches were packed, that we had contributed to the 401(k)s and that our investments were properly allocated between fixed income and stocks. That the kids had 529 plans for college. All this stuff. We were building this thing one block at a time. And he pulls that all down?"

"Why did he do that?" Sandy said.

"Just look at him," Gretchen said. "He did it because he was unhappy. He's unhappy. Look."

"Why?" Sandy said, thinking that Gretchen was doing just what she wanted Gretchen to do: look at Steve.

Sandy also saw Gretchen going up to the line. Gretchen did not like to go into unknown emotional territory, and she was about to go there; she hesitated on the edge.

"It wasn't enough for him," Gretchen said, shaking her head. "He had everything and it wasn't enough. I'm not the romantic, Steve is the romantic. He couldn't deal with the ordinary, humdrum, take the bucket up the hill and then do it again. He had to have the beautiful princess."

"You say Steve couldn't deal with the humdrum, take the bucket up the hill again and again," Sandy said. "Okay. So, he couldn't do that. But don't a lot of people hate their jobs and want to change?"

"He had the best job, he had the most important job, he made the most money, as he kept saying," Gretchen said. "Give me a break."

"He hated his job," Sandy said. "He was jealous of you, because you loved yours."

It stopped Gretchen cold. Steve had been jealous of her? She'd never thought of that, and now she did. There was something appealing about how a new thought could stop Gretchen in her tracks.

"Steve jealous of me? Come on," Gretchen said. She did this thing with her hands, as if she were in class, a big gesture, so it could reach the big audience in the classroom, her arms coming in, folded across her chest, and was shaking her head.

"Would you do Steve's job?" Sandy said.

"Not in a minute," Gretchen said. Honestly.

"And he had to?" Sandy said.

Gretchen suddenly smiled.

"He wanted to," Gretchen said. "He loved it."

"Why?" Sandy said.

"You see Steve's watch?" Gretchen asked.

"Yes," Sandy said.

"That watch is a Rolex Submariner," Gretchen said. "I bought it for Steve years ago. He wanted one so bad and we couldn't afford it then. But he wanted to look cool, like the other guys at the firm. He wanted to be part of the team. So I got it for him."

Gretchen looked at Steve.

"Yes, I'm looking at you, as Sandy tells me to do. You look sad," Gretchen said tentatively. "That watch was what you wanted, wasn't it? It made you happy?"

"I thought so at the time," Steve said slowly. "But then it didn't. I couldn't find a way to get off the train. It never stopped."

These two, they talk all the time in metaphors, Sandy thought. Luckily one of them was an English professor.

"What train?" Sandy asked.

"The everything train," Steve said.

"Which means? Steve, look," Sandy said. "There is a complicated railway system running around your brain. Or maybe it's like the New York subway system. You've got tracks crossing over each other, running parallel, then doubling back. So tell me the train you couldn't get off. The A train? The M? Were you going to the Bronx? Brooklyn? Manhattan?"

"I don't think that's right," Steve said. "There was only one train, my family, my job, the kids, Gretchen. They were all wrapped up together."

Of course he was right, Sandy realized.

The session was already ten minutes over time. No, there wasn't another client waiting nervously in the little waiting room. Sandy was willing to go over time; if they needed to she was willing to go way over time.

But she had a feeling that they needed to think over what had happened in this session. Wouldn't it be better to leave it all at Steve's answer, incomplete as it was? Wouldn't that be something for them to mull over?

Sandy thought: Maybe Steve hadn't even been riding in his own train, he'd been on Gretchen's train, maybe you were the engineer, Gretchen, you decided where the train went. Maybe, Steve, you didn't have any way to stop Gretchen's train except to blow it all up.

21.

Each time it's different, Sandy thought. The next time always seems to be about something else, and then you realize it isn't.

"I'm sorry," Sandy said. "What is the Tactile Dome?"

"It's a semicircular mound with a passage that curls around inside it," Steve said. "The passage is lined with different surfaces. You crawl around in the dark and experience different touch sensations. You climb, you slide. The passage opens up, closes, but you can't see anything. It's really black.

"Anyway, it's at the Exploratorium. You can rent it for birthdays. Chris's whole class can come."

They were talking about their son Chris's birthday. He would be six.

Steve looked again at Gretchen. She shrugged.

"I'm not really up for a birthday party with Chris's whole class," she said. "I know that's what most people do, but it doesn't appeal to me. That doesn't mean you shouldn't do it."

"Aren't we doing this party together?" Steve said.

"I don't know," Gretchen said. "I don't think we have to. You're good at organizing stuff. You could just go ahead and do whatever you want. I could have time alone with Chris afterward. Maybe Liz could stay on with you and I could take Chris out to dinner, just him and me."

Sandy saw confusion and then disappointment sweep over Steve. He was let down, he went down as if he were sliding down a steep hill.

It's okay, Steve, Sandy thought. Birthday parties are really hard when you're separated, everything up in the air.

"What will Chris think if you're not there?" Steve said.

"He'll think that his parents are separated," Sandy said. "But I doubt he'll even notice. They all get such a sugar rush, all of them running around, everything a blur."

"I don't want to do this alone," Steve said quietly.

"You wouldn't be alone, you'll have twenty kids and twenty parents," Gretchen said. "Maybe Gabrielle will help you out."

"I'm going to ignore that," Steve said.

"Why?" Sandy said. "Why would you ignore it?"

Steve looked at Sandy, and then back to Gretchen.

"I'm not having an affair with Gabrielle," Steve said.

"Not yet," Gretchen said.

"Steve," Sandy said. "What did you feel when Gretchen said Gabrielle will help you out?"

"Like she was messing with me," Steve said.

"She was, but how did that make you feel?" Sandy said.

"What do you expect?" Steve said angrily. "I'm trying to make a plan for the birthday party. And this is what she throws at me? I should do it with Gabrielle? I felt angry."

"Fair enough," Sandy said. "And why do you think Gretchen said that Gabrielle would be glad to help you?"

"She's mad at me," Steve said.

"Okay," Sandy said. "And why is she mad?"

"Wait a minute," Gretchen said. "I'm not mad. I'm just sad, melancholy. I'm sorry."

Sandy took them back.

"Why won't you celebrate Chris's birthday with Steve?" Sandy asked.

"Good question," Gretchen said. "My feelings are complicated, but it's something like this: I realize that when you get divorced, there is a lot of pretending necessary to keep things on an even keel. You pretend at birthday parties, at graduations, at school events. But I don't want to pretend right now. I guess I don't want to learn how to pretend yet."

"I don't want to learn how to pretend either," Steve said.

"If I'm not at the party, then you won't have to," Gretchen

said. "You can just be Steve, Chris's father. You won't have to pretend to be Gretchen's husband."

"Why don't you want to learn how to pretend?" Sandy said.

"Who would?" Gretchen said.

"Someone who was getting a divorce," Sandy said. "That's what you told us."

"I *don't* want to get a divorce," Gretchen said vigorously. "Who ever wants to get a divorce? I would be crazy to want a divorce. One of the reasons I'm still here is that I don't want a divorce. But will I get divorced? I have no idea. You tell me. You have a lot of experience with couples on the brink."

"And I've been divorced," Sandy said. "And I can tell you that you don't want one if you can avoid it."

"How long ago did you get divorced?" Gretchen said. Then: "Is it okay if I ask that?"

"You can ask anything you want," Sandy said. "I don't do the therapist-must-keep-her-distance thing. I got divorced twenty-five years ago."

"You were married young," Gretchen said.

Sandy smiled. Divorced young, remarried young.

"Both times," she said.

Everything stopped for a moment.

"So I asked, will I get divorced?" Gretchen said.

"I don't know," Sandy said.

"Can I say something?" Steve said. "I don't want to get divorced."

Gretchen looked at him. She sort of drew herself together and thought for a moment before she said anything.

"But you cheated on me. Then you slept with Bonny Garvey," Gretchen said. "I'm not saying that was wrong. As Sandy says, I don't do wrong. But it still hurts me. I know that's crazy. I shouldn't be hurt. I left you. What are you supposed to do? And I have certainly not been faithful to you during our separation. Nevertheless, it still hurts me. And let's face it: you're on the verge of having an affair with Gabrielle, if you aren't having one already. I understand that. I know you're lonely and your ego has been hurt.

"But the thing is, the more time goes on, the longer we are separated, there are more and more hurts. We'll keep piling them on, until one day we crack. Then we get divorced."

"Everyone gets hurt, whether they are married or divorced," Sandy said. "The key is being able to handle it, deal with it."

"I'm not so sure," Gretchen said. She looked at Steve again. "I have this thing going with Bill. Not like it was before. But I like to talk to him. I like to get letters from him. Old-fashioned letters. On good paper. He writes them with a fountain pen and he has beautiful handwriting. How would you feel if we got back together and I still kept in touch with Bill? I probably wouldn't see him that much, just at the occasional conference. Could you handle that if we lived together, Steve? I don't want to be with him. I'm past that."

"At the occasional conference," Steve said. "Would you sleep with him?"

"I don't know," Gretchen said. "Probably not. But I certainly wouldn't make any promises."

"Are you serious about this?" Steve said.

Gretchen leaned forward and stared him in the eyes.

"I'm deadly serious," she said, sounding deadly serious.

Sandy guessed that when Steve felt very good about himself, when he was confident in himself, then he might take Gretchen up on this offer. But when he was down, when he was tired, insecure, had doubts about himself, then he would imagine that Gretchen was sleeping with Bill, and he would throw it back at Gretchen.

Steve now was in no condition to live with Gretchen on these terms, to be forever wondering if she was talking to Bill, writing to him, or sleeping with him. Steve wouldn't last twenty-four hours.

"I don't know," Steve said. "What if we lived together and I didn't make any promises about how I would act if you kept in touch with Bill?"

"Then we won't live together," Gretchen said. "I refuse to be beaten up emotionally."

Sandy realized that Gretchen was talking about the birthday party. Did Steve? If he didn't, Sandy would let him know.

"When have I done that?" Steve said.

"You're doing it right now," Gretchen said with feeling,

angry now. "About the birthday. You won't let me alone about it. I'm a bad person because I won't do what you think is right for the kids."

Sandy thought how amazing it was that you could put it all out there in front of a guy and he wouldn't, couldn't see it. It is right there, Steve, you have got to learn to see it. You have to.

"Steve, what is Gretchen saying to you?" Sandy said.

"She won't do a birthday party," Steve said quietly and tentatively, knowing that he didn't really understand.

Steve looked lost, in the middle of a forest that had no roads, asking, How had he gotten there if there were no roads?

"Gretchen said that you were beating her up about the birthday party," Sandy said. "From the beginning, she was saying that something was wrong about the birthday party. She was hurting about the birthday party. Why? And what does it have to do with Bill?"

She could see Steve's eyes, his mind, beginning to replay the session, to spin the tape back and then forward. Yes, Steve, it is that hard. But you can do it. Sandy wanted to throttle him, jump up, grab his head, and twist it.

"Steve!"

"Okay," Steve said. "Are you telling me that Gretchen feels so badly about us being separated that she doesn't want to parade it around in front of Chris's whole class?"

"I'm not telling you anything," Sandy said. "Ask Gretchen. It's about Gretchen's feelings."

Steve paused, thinking, an idea sliding over his face.

"And she thinks maybe Bill was a mistake and she's worried that I'll always be critical of her for that?" Steve said, beginning to really understand. The opposite of what she's said . . .

Steve looked at Gretchen. He got nothing back. She was too proud. And she wasn't any more in touch with her feelings than Steve was with his. Not yet.

"Ask Gretchen," Sandy said.

"Gretchen?"

"It tears my heart out that we have reached this point with the kids," Gretchen said softly. "They know what's going on."

"So let's find a solution that works for everyone," Steve said suddenly. He was on a roll, moving from idea to idea, finally beginning to see behind the words. Sandy watched as the new idea flooded into Steve.

"Chris loves trains," Steve said. "He has a huge wooden train set."

He smiled.

"How about this," Steve said. "We take Chris on a train ride to Palo Alto and back. His first ride on a real train. He can take one friend from class with him. Liz comes and she can bring a friend. We have a birthday lunch in Palo Alto."

Gretchen nodded.

"I like that." She thought for a moment.

"I can do that," she said.

22.

"So how did the birthday party go?" Sandy asked.

"It was pretty good," Steve said. "The kids enjoyed it."

He looked at Gretchen. Clearly he preferred that she be the one to talk about it.

"It was fine," Gretchen said evenly.

She looked over at Steve, then back at Sandy.

"Okay, that wasn't fair," Gretchen said. "Steve did a great job, he brought engineers' caps for the kids, and presents for everyone. He'd arranged for a picnic."

Gretchen seemed to draw into herself; she looked off into the middle distance.

"I don't think we've ever talked about it, but the weekend after that time I met Bill at the conference, I went with Steve and the kids to a friend's house in Palo Alto. They have two kids about the same age as Chris and Liz, and they have a big pool. We had arranged this a month before. How could I get out of it?

"Of course, the last thing I wanted to do was to spend a day with Steve and the kids, with these friends, and have to act as if I cared about Steve, or that we were still a family. I hated the whole idea of it. I felt numb in the car as we drove down. I would look over at Steve and I knew that he would never make me happy, that I would never have the connection with Steve the way I'd had this instant, overwhelming connection with Bill.

"It was the saddest day, and also so edgy. I was just repulsed to be with Steve, to think that he was the father of my kids, that I'd ever thought I'd loved him, that I'd ever made love with him.

"Now we were going back to Palo Alto, albeit on the train, not in the car, but still. So I thought about that other trip, when I really couldn't abide Steve and I believed that I would be able to make a life with Bill, telling myself that getting divorced wasn't so bad. That was eight months ago, and now on this trip, on the train, I could look at Steve, and I could appreciate the effort he'd put into this party. And

I could appreciate how he keeps coming, you know what I mean? I must have told him fifty times that I didn't want to do the birthday party with him, but he kept pushing it, pushing, and finally we reached this train compromise. And the kids had fun, and even I had fun."

Sandy was thinking that Gretchen had started out stonewalling the question of what the train trip party had been like. And then she'd been able to call out to her current feelings and her memories of her past feelings, and the feelings and memories had cocked their heads and had come bouncing back to her, like big shaggy dogs.

23.

"I just thought I'd let you know that I'm going to be out of town this weekend," Steve said. "But if you need backup, my parents are here."

"Where are you going?" Gretchen asked.

"Mendocino," Steve said.

"I hope you're not going to Mendocino with Bonny," Gretchen said. "That would tick me off."

"I haven't seen Bonny in months," Steve said. "I thought I told you that."

"Good," Gretchen said.

He was so comfortable in her office now, Sandy thought. She wanted them both to feel as if it were completely normal to talk about the most intimate things while she was in the room with them, where she was this little machine that could translate what they'd said into what they'd meant.

"So who are you going with?" Sandy asked.

"I'm going with Gabrielle," Steve said. "The woman who is my cooking teacher."

"You know, Steve," Gretchen said. "I actually do recall that you are being taught to cook by an Italian woman named Gabrielle. And you'll remember my curiosity got the better of me and I looked at her website. Isn't she about twenty?"

"No, she's in her thirties," Steve said.

"The cooking lessons must be going really well," Gretchen said.

"I'm available to make you dinner anytime," Steve said.

"But not this weekend," Gretchen said.

"This is the first time I've really done anything with her," Steve said.

"It's funny how last weekend we did the birthday party and this coming weekend you're going away with Gabrielle," Gretchen said.

"Why is that peculiar?" Sandy said. "You had a good time with Steve at the birthday and now he's going away with Gabrielle for a weekend. Why is it funny? What is the connection?"

"I'm referring to the irony of it," Gretchen said. "I have the first good time I've had with Steve in years, and the next thing I know he's going away for the weekend with his cooking teacher."

"Why doesn't that make perfect sense?" Sandy said.

"You mean that Steve spends the day with me, and then he wants to go away with another woman for the weekend? That makes sense?" Gretchen said. "One of the reasons I didn't want to do this birthday party with Steve was because I didn't want to send a message to the kids that we might get back together again."

"Really?" Sandy said. "You never mentioned that when we discussed the birthday plan. I don't think the kids have anything to do with this. I think you're unsure about Steve going away with Gabrielle because you're unsure about your relationship with Steve."

Gretchen sat up, shook her head.

"Yes, I'm unsure about Steve," she said. "But I'm unsure about almost everything right now."

Which is progress, Sandy thought.

"Do you want me not to go?" Steve asked.

"Steve, knock it off," Gretchen said.

"So how do you feel about it?" Steve said.

It occurred to Sandy that this was a pretty perceptive question, if a simple one, coming at this particular time.

"I don't know how I feel about it," Gretchen said. "I guess I'm happy that you are able to move on with your life. I'm glad you waited until after Chris's birthday party."

It was classic Gretchen; she said the exact opposite of what she felt. Move on with his life? Gretchen was happy? Gretchen, you are furious because Steve is going away with Gabrielle right after you had a good time with him at the birthday party.

"You don't sound happy," Steve said.

He got it. After eight months' work, he realized what was going on.

Gretchen shut her eyes.

"No, I'm not happy," Gretchen said. "I'm very lonely. I'm vulnerable. It's not a pretty picture. It's the middle of the winter, so I'm also cold."

"You always have trouble in the winter," Steve said.

"I should go skiing," Gretchen said. "Maybe I will."

You were perceptive and then you blew it, Steve, Sandy thought.

"Hold on a second, will you?" Sandy said. "Gretchen, you said you were lonely and vulnerable, and Steve, you said that Gretchen always has trouble in the winter." You were doing so well, Steve. "Steve, Gretchen just told you she was feeling lonely and vulnerable."

"I heard that," Steve said.

"Well, you're not acting like you hear her," Sandy said. "She says she's lonely, vulnerable. You don't follow up on that. And you were on a roll, Steve. Instead, you treat what

Gretchen said as if it were a sign of seasonal affective disorder. And then, Gretchen, you go along with Steve and start talking about skiing. You guys totally back away from the feelings that are lying there right in front of you. It's so scary to talk about feeling lonely and vulnerable that you retreat to the banal."

Sandy looked at Steve and Gretchen. They were in their mid-thirties, but at this moment they seemed much younger.

"Let's try this again, from the top," Sandy said. "You go, Gretchen. Your cue is that you're lonely and vulnerable."

Gretchen didn't say anything.

"Come on, Gretchen," Sandy said. "Humor me."

"I was feeling lonely and vulnerable," Gretchen said mechanically.

"Why?" Steve asked.

"Because I'm alone," Gretchen said. "And vulnerable."

"I thought you were going out with some friend of Lucy's, a writer," Steve said.

"Yes, I went out with him a few times, but he didn't make me feel happy," Gretchen said. "I burn through guys and none of them work for me."

"I don't like to hear that because it makes me jealous," Steve said.

"There's nothing to feel jealous about," Gretchen said. "I'd let you know if there was. I'm a nun at the moment. I tried to make myself feel something, but I never did. I'll be all right this weekend, though, because I have the kids."

"I have a question," Sandy said. "So Steve tells you he's going to Mendocino with Gabrielle, and immediately afterward you say that you're feeling lonely and vulnerable."

"I know there is a connection," Gretchen said.

"And you went on Gabrielle's website," Sandy said. "I mean, there is a lot of stuff going on here."

"Doesn't it seem a little odd that we spend so much time talking about other people we've been involved with," Gretchen said. "Is who you sleep with so important?"

"Well, it's the nominal reason that you guys got into trouble in the first place, but I agree that it's just a symptom, that the real troubles have to do with the lonely and vulnerable components," Sandy said. "You went on Gabrielle's website how many times? I know you went on it before. I remember you commenting on her eating a tomato. You went on it again, recently?"

"Yesterday," Gretchen said angrily.

"So Gabrielle's website has this really true, and accurate portrait of her?" Sandy said.

In spite of feeling lonely and vulnerable, Gretchen actually smiled at this.

"Well, it has recipes that look pretty accurate," Gretchen said. "She has a clip of her making raviolis. With the machine and everything. I've always wanted to try that. I watched and I thought, This is someone Steve is going to like."

"And?" Sandy said.

"On the website, she comes across as very likable," Gretchen said. "In a very Italian way. You know, the dark earth mother. I suppose I'm the blond, blue-eyed ice princess. That's how Steve sees it. In reality, I'm sure she's a super bitch and will make Steve's life miserable, but, you know, we keep coming to see you, Sandy, good for us, but one of these days, some Italian cook is going to cook a meal for Steve that makes him fall for her. And then this is done."

"I'm not going to fall for anyone," Steve said.

"What really makes me crazy is that I've made you so much better, and some beautiful Italian is going to get the benefit," Gretchen said. "Sometimes I wish I was ready to live with you again."

"But you're not?" Steve asked.

"No," Gretchen said.

"Why not?" Steve asked.

"That is a good question, a very good question," Gretchen said. "One reason is that I'm not ready to give up Bill."

Steve started to say something, but then he thought better of it, Sandy noticed.

"I mean, yes, I've given up on him in a sense, but I can't seem to get him out of my system. When he calls, it still knocks me over sometimes," Gretchen said.

"He is such a jerk," Steve said slowly.

"Agreed. But I was telling you how I feel. You should pay attention to that."

"Why does he knock you over?" Steve asked after a moment.

"When I met him, I was a damsel in distress," Gretchen said. "You remember when you and I went to Mendocino? That time when we left the kids with your parents? We rented kayaks and paddled up that river."

Sandy noticed how Gretchen dropped Bill. Sandy felt that Gretchen was about to switch to Gabrielle, that Gretchen had made a connection between the two.

"That was great," Steve said.

"So take Gabrielle up the river," Gretchen said.

Which was not what she meant. It wasn't close. It was the opposite of what she meant. Steve was just looking at Gretchen. He didn't say anything.

"Bill really hurts, doesn't he," Sandy said to Steve. "Why do you think Gretchen brought him up? What did she mean when she said she wasn't ready to give him up?"

She says the opposite of what she means . . .

Steve looked at Sandy and then back at Gretchen. Sandy saw the idea hit him. It literally pushed him back in his chair.

"I'm not going to fall in love with Gabrielle," Steve said. "It's a nice relationship, but it's not like what you had with Bill."

Steve paused for a moment.

Then he said: "I have an idea. You're talking about the fact that I'm going away for the weekend with Gabrielle. Why don't we plan a weekend away. For ourselves."

He got it, Sandy realized, he understood that Gretchen had given up Bill and didn't want him to come back as Gabrielle.

"Maybe we can talk about it after you get back from your weekend with Gabrielle," Gretchen said.

24.

"*So how was* your weekend with Gabrielle?" Sandy asked Steve, thinking it was a pretty obvious and not very creative start. But it was what she wanted to know.

Gretchen was looking out the window. Now she turned back and faced Sandy.

"Let's stop it right there," Gretchen said. "You told me that I was beating myself up by looking at Gabrielle's website. Fair enough. I agree. So I certainly don't want to hear that they had a great time and how the sex was."

"How do you know they had a great time?" Sandy said. "Or if they slept together?"

Gretchen shook her head. She turned her right hand palm up and raised it.

"It doesn't matter," Gretchen said. "I thought hard about this. Whatever happens outside this room doesn't matter."

"I don't understand what you're getting at," Steve said.

"You and me, our story?" Gretchen said. "It's what is going on right now, in this room. This is where it happens. This is what counts. If you're not here, in the room, you don't count. Gabrielle isn't here."

"But isn't the idea for us to learn stuff here that helps us in the real world?" Steve said.

"What real world?" Gretchen said. "Can I be honest with you, Steve?"

Gretchen turned to Sandy.

"I'm not asking Steve if I can be honest, I'm asking myself, as in do I dare to be really honest with Steve?"

"Sure you can," Sandy said.

"Okay, here goes," Gretchen said. "I spend a huge amount of my time in what you call the real world, thinking about what happens here, in the one hour a week I spend in this room with you and Sandy. My whole week is organized around this hour."

Steve nodded.

"I do too," he said.

"So I think there is a story going on here," Gretchen said. "Sandy may be creating it for us, or bringing it out in us. I'm not sure who is the real author."

"What kind of a story is it?" Sandy said.

"It's about Steve and me being vulnerable with each other," Gretchen said. "Being willing to take chances with each other. It's also about learning what we really feel, which is pretty hard to do."

"Right," Sandy said. "And it's also about changes you two have made in terms of how you lead your lives."

"You mean how Steve has turned into a good father," Gretchen said.

"Yes, that's part of it," Sandy said. "The other part is that you let him."

"Steve, do you get what I'm trying to say?" Gretchen said, looking at Steve. Her voice was pleading.

"I think I do," Steve said.

Gretchen said: "Months ago, when I went to that divorce lawyer? Remember?"

"Of course I remember," Steve said.

"I was so wired, so wrung out, so gutter," Gretchen said. "Should I divorce Steve? Should I get it over with? What was Steve going to do? What lawyer would he hire? Would his lawyer be tougher than mine? All these questions running through my mind. Now?"

Gretchen stopped. She shrugged her shoulders.

"Now, if you came in here and said, Gretchen, I went to see a lawyer, and I'm filing for divorce, I would say, Fine, Steve, if that makes you happy. But I wouldn't do anything about it. I wouldn't go to see a lawyer. As long as you were still coming here, I'd just let it go."

"What would you do if Steve stopped coming here and went to see a divorce lawyer?" Sandy said.

"Oh, let's go all the way," Gretchen said. "What would I do if Steve stopped coming here, saw a divorce lawyer, and then filed for divorce? Am I still coming here? Even if it's alone?"

"Sure," Sandy said. "If you wanted to."

"I would want to," Gretchen said. "So I wouldn't do anything. I'd just keep coming here and talking to you."

"Even if I filed for divorce?" Steve said.

"Oh, Steve," Gretchen said. "Come on. Work with me. What difference would it make if you filed for divorce? You think that would get you anywhere?"

"It would get us divorced," Steve said.

Gretchen looked at Sandy. "Is he ever going to get it?" she asked.

"I don't know," Sandy said. She looked at Steve.

"Do you want to get a divorce?" Sandy asked.

"Of course not," Steve said. "It's the last thing I want. I said that."

"But if you got a divorce what would change?" Sandy asked. "Would you still feel the same way?"

"It would end something. I mean, suppose Gretchen died, that would be the end of our relationship, wouldn't it?" Steve said. "What if Gretchen died and I got remarried? You're saying that wouldn't make any difference?"

"So, I have a friend," Sandy said. "She was with her husband in Africa. He worked for the UN. They got into a car accident. He was killed. She almost died. Now he comes back to her in her dreams. Every night. It's been going on for seven years. In her dreams, he rings the doorbell, or she hears him open the garage door. Now she writes down the dreams every morning."

"You're saying he died and nothing changed?" Steve asked.

"Not for her," Sandy said. "Her dreams are her therapy. You come to this office. She dreams."

Steve was looking intently at Gretchen.

"Steve, here's the thing," Gretchen added. "I'm saying that our time in this room *is* the real world. The stuff outside this room? Who knows?"

Gretchen smiled to herself. She was looking down. Then she looked up again, at Steve.

"Steve, this is also another way of saying that we had to let each other go," Gretchen said. "I've let you go."

"Now you lost me," Steve said. "I thought I was beginning to understand when Sandy talked about her friend whose husband had died."

"Remember at the beginning how Sandy was always

telling us that we had to let each other go?" Gretchen said. "She said there was this paradox. If we were ever going to get back together, we had to let each other go?"

"I remember that," Steve said. "And I never understood it."

"I didn't get it then either, but I think I'm beginning to," Gretchen said. She turned and looked at Sandy. "You meant that we had to give up trying to control each other. I could get Steve not to sleep with Gabrielle, but that would be useless, wouldn't it?"

"Yes," Sandy said. "It would."

"He is the one who has to decide what happens with Gabrielle, not me," Gretchen said. Now she turned back to Steve.

"Steve, what happens with Gabrielle? It's all your call," Gretchen said. "So, like with divorce, Sandy was saying that is just another method of one person in the relationship trying to control the other. Sandy is saying, even with the ultimate control, death, you still don't ultimately control. So don't even think about killing me, by the way, it won't change anything, I'll just come back to haunt you. Sandy is saying that what you do with Gabrielle is irrelevant until you are finished dealing with me. Are you finished with me?"

"No," Steve said. "Obviously I'm not, because I keep coming here, to this office week after week."

"And the fact that you go out with Gabrielle? It won't influence me one way or the other, it won't do anything to me, I don't care. I don't want to be controlled, I won't let her control me," Gretchen said.

"So anyway," Sandy said. "Steve? How was your weekend with Gabrielle?"

"If you mean, did we sleep together? No, we didn't," Steve said.

25.

It had come over Sandy gradually: a warm and affectionate feeling for both Gretchen and Steve, a belief that they were both decent, careful people. Sure, they'd lost their way, but that happened sometimes.

They had come in together—Steve holding the door open for Gretchen.

"Nice to see you," Sandy said. "Do we have any business to attend to this week before we get down to it? I mean practical stuff. Kids have scheduling issues? Job demands?"

"I have something," Steve said. "As you know, I've changed my relationship with my firm. I'm working three-quarter time, but I'm still an actual member of the firm and I've begun earning back my capital investment as well as earning a percentage of the firm revenues. I just received my first draw."

He had come in with a thin brown leather attaché case that had shiny bronze latches. Now he snapped them open and pulled out a manila folder.

"Anyway, half of the drawdown is yours," he said, holding out the folder to Gretchen.

She took the folder from him, opened it, looked at it, closed it, and handed it back to Steve.

"It's a lot of money," she said.

"Not really," Steve said.

"I still have the money from when we sold the house. I put it into a money market fund. It's sitting there. I've used less than twenty thousand," Gretchen said. "I'm not ready to deal with more money right now. There's too much going on."

"You need to deal with it sometime," Sandy said.

"For the time being, Steve can invest it for me," Gretchen said.

"I don't want to do that," Steve said. "I don't think I should."

Gretchen looked at him, as in, Why, Steve?

"At the very beginning, Sandy told us that I'd used money as a means of control," Steve said. "We are supposed to be letting go of each other."

"Do you want to let go of me?" Gretchen asked.

"You know I don't," Steve said.

"Then don't," Gretchen said. "Hold the money for me. You're good with money, you always have been. I realize I've given you trouble about it, but I appreciate your skill. Managing money just isn't something I want to have to learn about right now. But that doesn't mean I don't want money, that I want to live like a starving student or anything. I like nice things."

Sandy thought: It shows that you like nice things, Gretchen, but you don't advertise it. Gretchen was looking particularly beautiful this morning. But not expensive, not downtown. She wore old, gnarled black leather boots. A simple black skirt, with a plain white blouse. No jewelry, not even a watch. The only fancy thing was the brown leather bag from Bottega Veneta, which Steve had bought her. She was clean, simple, straightforward. Now Sandy noticed the diamond studs in her ears, large and beautiful stones, hiding in the straw of her long blond hair. So there was some jewelry after all, but you had to find it,

"I know how to do a spreadsheet," Gretchen said, and smiled. And then Steve smiled back at her.

In this instant, Sandy thought, they were together, as together as any couple anywhere, except for the broken clocks in their hearts.

But Sandy wasn't sentimental. She was into clock repair.

"You could take a course in investing," Sandy said.

"I don't want to take a course in investing," Gretchen said. "That is the last thing in the world I want to take a course in. Sandy, after all this time? Are you kidding me?"

"Why not?" Sandy said. Her mother had made her take accounting her freshman year in college. Either that or Heidi wasn't paying tuition.

"I don't get it," Gretchen said. "I'm still married to Steve. Why shouldn't I get some benefit out of that? I live on my own, I run my life on my own. Why do I have to do everything? Steve is not going to lose the money."

"How do you know that?" Steve said.

"You wouldn't be able to sleep at night, I know you," Gretchen said.

"That's probably true," Steve said.

"You know, you have some useful qualities," Gretchen said. "And in some ways we are very complementary. But then I let you take our life and run away with it."

Gretchen shook her head.

"I'm sorry I didn't stop you," she said.

"I was pretty unstoppable," Steve said.

"You were, but we both made mistakes," Gretchen said.

Gretchen was all soft this morning, Sandy realized, a continuation of their last session.

"My husband and I have an investment advisor who runs our money, such as it is," Sandy said. "I could give you her name."

"Who is she?" Steve asked.

"Donna Logan at Bostick Davis," Sandy said.

"I don't know her, but I know the firm," Steve said.

"Sandy, what is the problem?" Gretchen said, irritated. "I have asked Steve to keep the money for me. Why are you trying to mess with that? We are always going to have some connections no matter what happens."

"As Steve said, the problem with that is that money is often an instrument of control," Sandy said.

"But do you remember, it was at one of our first sessions together, and I said I needed money because I was moving into my new flat and there were a lot of expenses? What happened? Steve handed over everything we got from selling our house in Ross."

Because I told him to, Sandy thought. And he did it because he realized if he didn't, you would divorce him then and there. But it was a very, very smart move on Steve's part. I give him that.

"I remember," Sandy said.

"Has anything like that happened with any of your other people?" Gretchen said.

"It was unusual," Sandy said.

Maybe Gretchen was right. For them money wasn't a problem. For Sandy it had always been an issue. Maybe she was blinded by that.

"You could be onto something," Sandy said. "When I think about it, we haven't spent any time dealing with money. It's never seemed to be a problem."

Of course, you guys have always had money, Sandy thought, you could do with knowing what it's like when you don't. As when my mother was on the verge of bankruptcy.

"Maybe we didn't argue about money because there always was some," Gretchen said. "But that was because of Steve."

Okay, Sandy thought, we're in sync. So let's explore this.

"I'm sure that's part of it. The fact that you have had money. But you know what I'm hearing?" Sandy said. "What I'm hearing is that you trust Steve. Is that what you're saying?"

Gretchen looked at Steve for a moment, and then turned back to Sandy.

"That's a good question, isn't it," Gretchen said. "Could it be possible that after nine months here, I've somehow begun to trust Steve again? I need to think about that. Are you lying to me about anything, Steve?"

"No," Steve said. "Not anymore."

"But you did," Gretchen said wistfully. "You lied a lot."

"And I'm so sorry," Steve said.

"Maybe you are sorry," Gretchen said. "Funny, I actually believe that you might be sorry."

"I am," Steve said.

Gretchen turned to Sandy.

"Here is Steve going out with his Italian cooking lady, Gabby. Here we are living separately. But here we are faithfully coming to your office every week, week after week."

"But here I am not sleeping with the Italian cook," Steve said.

"Yes, I do want to ask you about that," Gretchen said.

Now she leaned forward.

"Actually that is a great question, Sandy. Do I trust Steve?" she said. "Steve, I think you have made a good-faith effort here, in this office, with Sandy helping you out."

Gretchen turned to look at Sandy again.

"So, all in all, yes, I trust Steve," she said. "Amazing."

Now she turned to Steve.

"By the way, how are things going with Gabrielle?" she asked. "I know last time I said I didn't want to hear about your weekend. I said that all that counted was what happened in this office. Now I do want to hear. I just never know how I'm going to feel. Do you? So how is it going with Gabrielle?"

Steve didn't say anything for a moment. Finally . . .

"How is it going with Gabby? I enjoy her company," Steve said. "Is there anything specific you want to know? That would be easier to answer."

"Why didn't you sleep with her? Who goes away for a weekend in Mendocino with a beautiful earthy Italian babe and doesn't sleep with her?" Gretchen asked.

"Well, we made out," Steve said.

Sandy and Gretchen smiled. You used the joke to change the subject, Sandy thought; why didn't you answer Gretchen's question?

"Okay. What does Gabrielle think about all this?" Gretchen said. "How you are sleeping with her and going to marriage counseling week after week with your wife?"

"I haven't slept with her," Steve said. "I told you that."

"I know," Gretchen said. "I guess she doesn't want to sleep with you if you're still involved with your wife. As in coming here."

"That's part of it," Steve said.

Of course Gretchen remembered that Steve had said he hadn't slept with Gabrielle, Sandy thought. Gretchen is taking you somewhere, can you see it, Steve?

"Oh, Steve," Gretchen said, and she leaned toward him. "It's hard, isn't it? Really hard."

"She thinks I ought to divorce you," Steve said suddenly, honestly. "She has a sort of cut-and-dried attitude. She doesn't tolerate a lot of ambiguity."

For the first time, Steve had thrown Gabrielle into the room. Not the dark-haired beauty of the Internet, but the Gabrielle he actually knew. This was progress, and Gretchen had brought it on.

"That's what you wanted to hear, wasn't it?" Steve added.

"I did want to hear what Gabrielle was thinking about you and me," Gretchen said.

"So why the hell didn't you just ask me?" Steve shot back.

"I did ask you," Gretchen said. "And I was proud of myself for daring to ask you. You just didn't hear me. I made real progress. Why didn't you hear me ask?" She paused and then suddenly lit up. "I know why. Because I screwed it up by pretending that I assumed that Gabrielle had slept with you, even though you told me that you hadn't slept with her. I'm sorry. I make things so complicated sometimes I can't unravel them. I thought you might be lying to me. But I'm trying to learn to be better."

"It's okay," Steve said.

"No, it's not okay," Gretchen said.

Everything seemed to stop for a moment. Finally, Sandy said to Gretchen: "So what do you think about Gabrielle wanting Steve to divorce you?"

"That Gabrielle wants Steve to divorce me?" Gretchen said.

"Yes," Sandy said.

"Well, it's a bummer," Gretchen said. "But then what did I expect? I mean, love is sort of take no prisoners. But what really hit me was that Gabrielle can't tolerate ambiguity." She looked at Steve. "And she's still fun to go out with?"

What a good question, Sandy thought. Ambiguity is our stock-in-trade here.

"In some ways it's refreshing," Steve said.

I'll bet, Sandy thought. But fairly limiting.

"I'll bet," Gretchen said. "What a change of pace for you."

In sync, Sandy thought.

Steve started to say something and then stopped. Sandy tried to think what it might have been, but she couldn't quite grab Steve's thought.

In sync with Gretchen, but not Steve.

"Do you like Gabrielle a lot?" Gretchen asked.

"Yes, I like her a lot," Steve said.

But not enough, Sandy thought.

"I feel threatened," Gretchen said. "I'm not kidding. I thought you were madly in love with me."

"I am madly in love with you," Steve said. "I have developed an ability to tolerate truckloads of ambiguity."

Sandy saw the tears falling slowly and handed Gretchen the tissue box.

26.

"Thanks for seeing me alone," Gretchen said.

Sandy thought that Gretchen looked better all the time. She didn't seem jumpy anymore, as if on the lookout for something to come at her. She had managed to work out a life on her own, and she had a relationship with Steve that was complicated, difficult, but, Sandy also thought, a relationship that could be trusted. He might be about to sleep with the tricky, and Sandy thought conniving, Gabrielle, but Gretchen knew about it and everything else.

Sandy thought, Now they are apart, now they are seeing other people, but now, in their own strange way, they trust each other more than when they were together.

"Anyway," Gretchen said. "Remind me what the deal is in these private meetings. Does everything we say privately have to go back to the other person?"

"I don't know," Sandy said. "Whatever it is, why don't you just share it with Steve? I am really in favor of you guys telling each other stuff. Rather than me doing it."

Gretchen looked over at the green chair. The marriage is there, Sandy thought, and you see it.

Gretchen seemed to be thinking this over.

"So what's up, Gretchen?" Sandy said, prodding her.

"I guess I could tell Steve this if I had to," Gretchen said. "I've been thinking about how to explain this to you, and I think the way to go is to share something with you."

She pulled the Bottega Veneta bag into her lap and reached inside. She held something out to Sandy. Sandy took it. It was a Valentine's Day card. On the outside, in sweeping script, it read: Love: the greatest blessing. Sandy opened it. The message on the inside read: Feeling so grateful for you on Valentine's Day. It was signed "Bill."

Gretchen reached into the magical chocolate-colored brown bag again and came out with something else, which she handed to Sandy. It was a small silver bud vase, very simple, maybe Scandinavian, maybe antique Georg Jensen, Sandy wasn't sure. It was delicate and obviously expensive.

"And one thing more," Gretchen said.

The last thing Gretchen handed to Sandy was a very small watercolor painting, not even four inches across. It was a simple landscape, a beach, the ocean, and far out, a sailboat flying a spinnaker, which was in the shape of a heart. At the bottom, there were words From a secret admirer.

"I've got some ideas, but I think it would help if you explained these to me," Sandy said.

"Okay," Gretchen said. "As you know it was Valentine's Day last week. The card is from Bill. The vase and the picture are from Steve."

"Your secret admirer," Sandy said. "There was a rose in the vase?"

"That would be too obvious for Steve," Gretchen said. "Freesia. Yellow freesia, a single stem."

"I like the bud vase," Sandy said honestly. It was beautiful.

"I like it too," Gretchen said. "I like this purse too. Steve is great at giving presents, and I don't just mean that they are expensive. He thinks about them."

"Tell me about the card," Sandy said.

"Just look at the contrast," Gretchen said.

"Tell me about it," Sandy said.

"It's tacky, what can I say?" Gretchen said. She paused.

"What am I trying to say? I'm judging someone on their Valentine's Day present? That sounds crazy, doesn't it?"

"Not to me," Sandy said. "How do you come out on this?"

"It's just a card. Bill is really earnest. He's the salt of the earth," Gretchen said.

He doesn't have any taste, Sandy thought, but Gretchen could probably teach him over time.

"But we're never going to get together," Gretchen said. "We just aren't. Even if he wasn't married, we wouldn't get together. I know that now."

Gretchen leaned forward and stared at Sandy.

"But that doesn't mean I don't care about him, I do. I needed him. He was really important to me," Gretchen said.

"Can we back up for a moment," Sandy said. "Before you showed me the valentine card, I had a different image of Bill. He's an English professor, he sends you letters that he writes with a fountain pen. I thought he was sophisticated."

"Look," Gretchen said. "Bill is the smartest guy to ever come out of a small town in western Wisconsin. He's created himself. It's not easy to do."

"I'm confused," Sandy said.

"Me too," Gretchen said.

"I think you're saying that you see Bill differently now," Sandy said.

"I do," Gretchen said. "It just isn't going to work out."

"But you knew it wasn't going to work out," Sandy said.

"You knew he was married. That he'd already been divorced once. I thought one of Bill's good points was that he was safe. You could just have an affair with him. Didn't have to worry about actually being with him."

What are we talking about, Sandy wondered. Something didn't make sense. Gretchen was a master of indirection. It was one of the biggest problems Sandy had with her. They needed to work on it.

Gretchen had taken them down one path, Bill's path. Sandy backed up to the crossroads and went down the other.

"What did you think when you got the valentine from the secret admirer?" Sandy asked.

"Okay, why the sailboat? When we were first in love, we talked about getting a sailboat and sailing off into the sunset, having a great romantic adventure. Across the Pacific. Steve is a great sailor, but then we had our careers and then the kids and we were working all the time. That's why he put the picture of the sailboat on the valentine. It had a message," Gretchen said.

"Which was?" Sandy asked.

"That we could still get the sailboat," Gretchen said.

"Do you want to get the sailboat?" Sandy asked.

"I don't know," Gretchen said slowly. "I hate to say it, but there is a part of me that does. I don't think it's the smart part of me."

"Why isn't it smart?" Sandy asked.

"It's romantic," Gretchen said. "And I've had it with romantic love." She looked at the green chair. "You talk about the marriage and how it's something you build up over time. It's like a brick wall, you build it one brick at a time. But romantic love is like a drug, you take it, and bam, you're there, you're in it. The problem is, then it wears off."

"Gretchen, it was Valentine's Day," Sandy said.

"Steve was like trying to pull this romantic love thing on me," Gretchen said. "Does he think I'm going to fall for it again?"

"It was Valentine's Day," Sandy said. "Did you want him to give you a cordless power drill?"

"But the sailboat," Gretchen said.

"Can I see the picture again?" Sandy said wearily.

Gretchen handed it to her.

"So I would have to say that Steve is pretty good at watercolors," Sandy said. "I couldn't do this, and I've taken lessons."

"He is good," Gretchen said. "His mother is a painter. Well, she paints."

"So, looking at this picture, the sailboat is in the distance, there is a beach in the foreground, then ocean, clouds," Sandy said. "The sailboat seems to be moving away from us. It's dissolving in the marine layer. It's about to disappear. That suggests to me that Steve's message is complex. He's aware of romantic love, but he sees that it inevitably dissolves. But that doesn't mean you can't have a great vacation at this beach, with the kids, in Hawaii or Mexico."

"Are you making fun of me?" Gretchen said.

"Or you don't take the kids on the vacation," Sandy said. "Yes. A little maybe. Making fun of you. Which leads me to another question: Have you come to any conclusion about going away with Steve for a weekend?"

Which is exactly what this Valentine's watercolor is about, Sandy thought, and why Gretchen is here talking to me.

"A strange thing happened to me last week," Gretchen said. "That stupid drama professor I went out with a few months ago, the one who wouldn't let me alone? I let him come over. And then I slept with him."

"Okay," Sandy said.

"Why did I do that? He wasn't important to me," Gretchen said. "And frankly I don't like sleeping around either. Believe it or not."

"I do believe that," Sandy said. "So why did you do that?"

"This is going to sound crazy, but I think it had to do with Steve," Gretchen said.

Life is a puzzle, isn't it? Sandy thought. Valentine's Day, the picture, the bud vase, the one-night stand. How do they all fit together? Sandy didn't try to push Gretchen to bring it all together. Maybe it was enough that she could see that they all had to do with Steve and the weekend.

Enough? Sandy saw how much progress that was, how far Gretchen had come to be able to see that it all had to do with Steve.

"If I go away with Steve for a weekend, I'm not going to sleep with Steve," Gretchen said.

"Yet you just slept with someone casually," Sandy said.

"It wasn't casual," Gretchen said stiffly.

"Well, what was it?" Sandy asked.

"I don't know," Gretchen said. "He was there when I realized I didn't love Bill. He helped me when I was down. And, frankly, maybe I did it because he didn't count."

No, Sandy thought. If that were true, you wouldn't be telling me about it.

"They all count," Sandy said. "Every single one of them. You slept with this guy you don't care about because you do care about Steve. I don't know exactly why this guy, at this time, and how it connects with Steve, but it does. Because you're angry at Steve? Scared of Steve? Want to hurt Steve? Or something else entirely. But believe me, it was about Steve."

There were tears now in Gretchen's eyes. She grabbed a tissue before they reached her face.

"You're right," Gretchen said. "It was all about Steve. And I don't want to tell Steve about it."

"Gretchen, why don't you make it easy on yourself?" Sandy said. She was resigned, and she sounded that way. World-weary.

"Just tell him, will you?" Sandy said. "Not tomorrow, perhaps, but you'll know when it's right."

"Okay," Gretchen said. "I will."

"Good," Sandy said. And suddenly she got it. Of course.

"I know why you slept with the professor," Sandy said.

"Yes," Gretchen said. "So do I. I just figured it out. I was saying goodbye to him. I said goodbye to him because I'm going to do the weekend with Steve. I was saying goodbye to all of it."

"It's time," Sandy said.

"But it doesn't mean I'm getting back together with Steve!" Gretchen said, leaning forward, suddenly angry. And then the wave passed over her.

"Of course not," Sandy said. "By the way, what do you think Steve gave Gabrielle for Valentine's Day?"

"Excuse me? You're evil today," Gretchen said. "Why would I care about that?"

"You wouldn't," Sandy said. "Because you know that there is no way he put half as much thought into that gift as he did into his gift for you."

27.

Sandy looked at Gretchen's beautiful bag, the one from Bottega Veneta that Steve had given her. It was a deep buttery brown, large like a lawyer's bag. Usually Gretchen casually dropped it on the floor and ignored it, but today she'd carefully moved it close to her chair, as if she were protective of it.

Sandy looked at Steve. Steve was looking out the window. Through it, you saw the top of the tall pepper tree, and now there were finches hopping in its branches.

Gretchen, why are you so protective of the bag? Sandy wondered. What's in it?

Suddenly the bag moved. There was something in it, alive, moving. As if there was a snake, a cobra, in the purse.

Gretchen saw it too.

"I put my phone on vibrate," she said. Pulled the bag into her lap, opened it, looked in, took out her phone, looked at the message, turned the phone off, tossed it back into the bag, closed the bag, put it back close to her, on the floor.

"Sorry," Gretchen said. "I meant to turn it off."

Which you have done every session for months. What is it now, Gretchen? Why was it not turned off?

Marriage counseling: they came to her office serious, and completely prepared. They never left a phone on unless they wanted it on.

And then Sandy knew. How? Who knows? She had been sitting with this unusual woman, this talented, brilliant . . . Anyway, Sandy knew.

"Call this an educated guess," Sandy said, looking at Gretchen. "I'm wondering. Do you have a letter from Bill in your bag?"

It was as if she'd slapped Gretchen. Her face went red; her eyes darted at Sandy.

"What I have in my bag is private," Gretchen snapped. "And what I share is my decision."

"Yes it is," Sandy said. "Let's talk about your decision. Why don't you want to share what's in your bag?"

"I didn't say I had a letter in my bag," Gretchen said. Sandy heard it as an admission that she did.

"Then let's just pretend you do," Sandy said. "You wouldn't share it? I'm asking why."

They looked at each other. Gretchen knew this would happen, Sandy thought. Give her time to play it out.

"Steve and I are living apart. We have our own lives. It's very important for me to keep myself separate from Steve," Gretchen said.

Come on, Gretchen, Sandy thought, not that again.

"Why did you bring the letter here today?" Sandy asked.

Gretchen pushed out her hands, palms up.

"I brought my notebooks, my notes for my lectures, my cell phone, my wallet," she said. "I brought what I was working on."

"You were working on Bill's letter?"

"Okay," Gretchen said, hesitating. "I do have a letter from Bill. But I haven't opened it."

"Why haven't you opened it?" Sandy asked.

"I didn't have time," Gretchen said.

"Really? You didn't have time?" Sandy said, eyebrows arched. She looked at Steve, who was looking intently at Gretchen.

Take it easy, Sandy, she reminded herself. This was progress, a lot of progress. Gretchen had brought Bill into the room, into their discussion. He could be sitting in the green chair. Gretchen wasn't quite ready to have Bill there, fully be there. Right now he was sort of a ghost. But . . .

"Why haven't you opened the letter?" Sandy asked again.

Gretchen was baffled. All the stuff she used to do, it didn't work. Nothing worked. A giant step: she was ready to give up trying to do that stuff. They were closer, Sandy thought.

"Of course I could have opened the letter," Gretchen said slowly. "So why didn't I? Good question."

Sandy let the *good question* hang there. Let them think about it. All of them. Steve, Gretchen, herself—and Bill in the green chair. Are you comfortable over there, Sandy thought, sitting in that big green chair with Steve and Gretchen's marriage? Apparently Bill was. He'd been sitting there a long time.

"I know it was a big deal and hard for you guys to separate," Sandy said. "And I think you did a very good job of disentangling from each other. That was not so easy. But now that you've done that, and you've been exploring each other again, I think it's time that you began exploring how to be intimate with each other."

"Okay, but we still have to have some limits," Gretchen said. "I have really fought hard to have my own space."

Sandy shook her head.

"Gretchen, can we cut through the no-trespassing signs," Sandy said. "Why don't you want to share Bill's letter?"

"But I haven't even read it," Gretchen said evenly.

"Yes, because you chose not to read it," Sandy said.

"Why does that matter?" Gretchen said.

"Why does that matter?" Sandy said. "Because you used to want to edit what Steve reads or sees. But now you're not so sure."

Sandy saw that now Steve was hanging on Gretchen's every word.

"Just humor me, Gretchen," Sandy said. "Right now, I'm just asking you why you don't want to share the letter with me or with Steve."

"First of all, there is a question of privacy," Gretchen said. "I didn't write the letter. It's Bill's letter. It would be his decision as to whether anyone read it."

"I see, so this is a question of Bill's rights or something?" Sandy said. "Let's just pretend for a moment that Bill is here with us, sitting right over there in the green chair."

"I thought the green chair was for the marriage," Gretchen said.

Sandy wondered, Does Gretchen see the marriage sitting in the green chair?

"Let's just put Bill in it for a moment," Sandy said. "Maybe the marriage is sitting in the green chair with him."

Amazingly, both Steve and Gretchen looked at the green chair. Sandy smiled, she couldn't stop herself.

"Can I say something?" Steve said.

"You don't have to ask permission," Gretchen said. Like the teacher she was.

But sometimes you do, Sandy thought. There was a reason Steve asked permission.

"I think Bill has been sitting in the middle of our marriage for a long time," Steve said.

He had asked permission because he was about to let his anger speak. He was saying, The son of a bitch has been hurting me.

His words produced an immediate reaction:

"You don't know anything about Bill," Gretchen said. "You know almost nothing about me either."

But there was no conviction in Gretchen's words. They were rote.

Let's back the train up, Sandy thought. It had been moving along so well, but the engineers between Gretchen's and Steve's ears had switched it to a trunk line that went nowhere.

Sandy felt it was better to take them back and put them on more or less solid ground.

"Now, what would Bill think about sharing his letters with Steve?" she asked.

Sandy gave them a concrete question that took them away from the hurt that Steve had laid out. They would have to deal with that, but when they were ready.

"Obviously he would be against it," Gretchen said. "It expresses private feelings that were meant to be shared only between Bill and me."

"He doesn't want to share his private feelings?" Sandy asked. "Why?"

"That seems self-evident," Gretchen said. "Private feelings are the ones that you don't share."

"I don't feel like running around in a circle," Sandy said. "You talk to Bill about what happens here, what happens in this room, right?"

Of course she did. Sandy saw Gretchen flinch, knowing where this was going.

"You share with Bill the most private things that happen in here, don't you? You have no trouble with that, right?" Sandy went on. "This isn't really about sharing private things, is it?"

"You tell me what it's about, then," Gretchen said evenly, on the verge of anger.

"I'll try. It's about intimacy. You're scared of being intimate with Steve, and for good reason. He hurt you. That was terrible, but you're getting over it. Now, Bill, look at him."

Sandy looked over at the green chair in the corner. She flicked her hand in its direction.

"He's almost a thousand miles away. And he's married. How is he going to hurt you? He's about as safe as it comes. So you can open up to him, and being that he has nothing to lose, he's never critical, never angry," Sandy said.

Now she looked over at Steve.

"Whereas this guy, he's all kinds of potential trouble. There is a fundamental difference between this guy," Sandy said, looking at Steve, "and that guy." She looked over at the green chair.

"Which is?" Gretchen said.

"This one," Sandy said, pointing a finger at Steve. "This one is real. Whereas the one in the green chair is imaginary."

"Bill isn't imaginary," Gretchen said in a low, rumbling voice.

"Oh, I think he is," Sandy said. "But let's just suppose that you shared his letter with Steve, and you just didn't tell Bill about it. How would that be?"

"I lie to Bill?" Gretchen said. "Is that what you're suggesting?"

"Sure," Sandy said. "Why not?"

"I thought you were all about telling the truth, that Steve and I were supposed to work on being honest with each other, that everything else flowed from that," Gretchen said.

"Being honest with each other—yes," Sandy said. "I didn't say anything about being honest with Bill. He doesn't seem to be particularly honest himself. At least, he's lying to his wife. For starters."

"So did Steve," Gretchen said. Hard.

"Yes, he did," Sandy said. "But he isn't lying now. Look at him. Do you think he's lying to you?"

Gretchen did look at Steve, and then back to Sandy. Then she looked at the green chair, then back at Steve, then at Sandy.

"No, now Steve's not lying," she said.

"Okay, now let me ask you something else," Sandy said. "Who do you trust? Steve, or the imaginary man in the green chair?"

"This is crazy," Gretchen said, angry. "This isn't marriage counseling. You're giving me the third degree while Steve just sits there brooding in his corner."

"Let's bring him in, then," Sandy said. "What do you think about all this?" she said to Steve.

"How did you know that Gretchen had a letter from Bill in her bag?" Steve said. Out of nowhere. Sandy didn't expect that.

"Intuition," Sandy said.

"Just intuition?" Steve said.

"Yes," Sandy said. "Would you like to read Bill's letter?"

"That's not my decision," Steve said carefully. "I respect Gretchen's privacy."

"Why do you respect that? What kind of relationship do you want?" Sandy said. "Do you want a relationship with a bill of rights? There are no rights in a relationship."

She said it too emotionally, too hard. A mistake.

"I asked if you would like to read the letter," Sandy said. "I wasn't handing it to you."

Steve paused.

"I think that reading the letter would probably hurt my feelings, but even so, it would mean that Gretchen trusted me," Steve said. "So yes."

"But I don't trust you," Gretchen said quickly. "I don't trust you with my feelings or my secrets. Anyway, don't you have secrets with Gabrielle?"

"We don't send letters, but you are welcome to read all my e-mails with her," Steve said quietly.

"She would say that was okay?" Gretchen said.

"Of course not," Steve said. "She'd be furious."

"So why are we talking about this?" Gretchen said to Sandy. "It's just going to cause pain."

Why did you bring Bill's letter? Sandy thought. Why hadn't you opened it? You created this whole thing, Gretchen. This is your doing. You wrote this session. You planned it.

"Yes, it is going to cause pain," Sandy said. "It's also going to be scary. But it's the only way to make this work. I want to do an exercise. It doesn't involve opening the letter. But I want you to take it out and show it to us."

Gretchen thought about it. And then she picked up her purse, opened it, looked inside, and pulled out a cream-colored envelope. She held it up. It was sealed, had never been opened. Her address was written in a beautiful sculpted script.

"Let Steve hold it," Sandy said.

Slowly, Gretchen handed the letter to Steve. He looked down at it as it rested in his hand.

"What are you feeling?" Sandy asked.

Still looking at the letter, Steve said: "Weird. I feel like I shouldn't be doing this, like I'm intruding."

"Why?" Sandy asked.

"It's between Gretchen and Bill," Steve said.

Give him time, Sandy thought. *Gretchen got it.*

"Not anymore," Gretchen said. "That's what Sandy's saying." She locked in on Steve.

"It's between you and me now," Gretchen said. The great big blue eyes holding him in their gaze. "That's the whole point of this exercise."

Steve looked at her. Did he understand?

"Look," Gretchen said. She pointed to the green chair. "Bill's been sitting there. He's been here with us. Sandy wants to throw him out. She wants the marriage to sit there, in the green chair. I've been sharing what we do in here with Bill. I've been telling him what's happening. Sandy's saying that has to stop. Instead, I share him with you. You. Me. No one else interferes. No one else comes into our room, this room. Our marriage sits in the green chair. Just the marriage."

Steve looked at the green chair and then back at Gretchen. He said nothing.

Gretchen blinked. Her eyes were full pools.

"I can't stand crying again," she said. "Fuck."

Sandy handed her the tissues.

"Okay, you're right," Gretchen said to Sandy. "You're right."

Then Gretchen turned to Steve:

"This letter is yours to read, Steve. I want you to read it. If you want to read all the letters Bill has written to me, you can do that too. I want you to read them all."

Gretchen had taken them apart, Sandy thought, and now she was putting them back together. If they fit back together. Maybe they didn't. But at least Gretchen was willing to see if they did.

Now everything focused on Steve. Two women looking at him as he held a letter from Bill. No one said anything for a while, almost a minute. Steve seemed to be thinking and Sandy let him. Then:

"I'm not much interested in reading what Bill writes to you," Steve said to Gretchen. "Why should I be? I'm interested in what you wrote to Bill. I care about what you think. Not him."

Yes, Steve, Sandy thought, good. But of course Steve cared about what Bill thought. Of course he felt competitive, of course he felt jealous.

It was clicking, Sandy thought, for both of them. Each leading the other one to the next step. If they got back together, she hoped they could remember this, when it all clicked. And when it wasn't working, that they could back the train up to this junction, to the switch, where it came apart, and go down the other track, to the one they were on now.

"I understand," Gretchen said quietly but with emotion. "I wish I had my letters to Bill so I could give them to you."

"So get them," Sandy said.

28.

"I read the letters," Steve said formally. "And I want to make some sort of statement about them, and even more about what is going on with you and me right now, Gretchen."

"You want to make a *statement*?" Gretchen said.

Steve smiled at her. *Smiled?* Sandy thought.

"*Statement* sounds sort of stilted, doesn't it?" he said. "Sorry about that. But about the letters. I don't feel angry. I don't even feel jealous."

"That's bighearted of you," Gretchen said. "Although I don't actually believe it. By the way, I went to a lot of trouble to get my letters back from Bill. He was surprisingly resistant and angry. But I got the letters. Now you've read them and you say you don't feel anything?"

"Oh, I feel a lot," Steve said. "I caused you a huge amount of pain. I feel really sorry about that."

"And reading the letters didn't cause you any pain?"

"Is that what you wanted me to feel?" Steve asked.

"I'm not sure," Gretchen said. Slow. "I was thinking a lot of different things. I still am. But yes, a part of me wants you to hurt, because of how much you hurt me."

"That was the big thing I saw in the letters," Steve said. "How much I hurt you. I'm so sorry."

He stopped to get himself ready for what was coming. Both Gretchen and Sandy looking at him, but neither saying anything . . .

"Another thing. I'm really grateful that you gave me these letters to read. You were trusting. In the old days, pre-Sandy, I would have hit the roof reading these love letters, feeling so betrayed. You trusted me not to do that. That's a very powerful statement."

Statement again. Sandy wondered why.

Gretchen cut in forcefully.

"Bill told me he had trusted me not to show his letters to anyone," Gretchen said. "He said that was our deal."

"And what did you say?" Sandy asked.

"What did I say?" Gretchen said. She turned to Sandy, as if surprised she were in the room. Wasn't it only Steve?

"I said that Sandy had told me to give them to you, and so he had to do it," Gretchen said. "I remembered how, our first time, Sandy told you to give me all the money from selling our house and you did it. But I didn't say that to Bill. Just that Sandy had said to give you the letters."

"But that didn't work, did it?" Sandy said. She knew.

Gretchen nodded at her.

"No, of course not," Gretchen said. "He sees you as a tool trying to get Steve and me back together. He said that he had trusted me to keep his love letters private. He said we had made a deal."

"But these were your letters you wanted," Sandy said.

"I know, he got mixed up," Gretchen said. "I straightened him out. I said how little his trust mattered to me, no matter whose letters they were. I said I was going to give Steve all the letters, mine and Bill's. I said I wasn't in the mood to cut a deal. I told him that there are no deals."

Gretchen looked at the green chair as if she were exchanging glances.

"Then he tried excuses," Gretchen said. "He said he had to keep the letters at his office and he didn't want to go into the office. Give me a break."

Gretchen sat up, as if to gird herself for what was coming.

"So the marriage sits in the green chair?" she said.

"It might," Sandy said. "I think sometimes it does."

"Well, the marriage told me to get the fucking letters and I made it clear to Bill that he had to give them to me or someone was going to send his letters to me to his wife."

Sandy wondered if Gretchen saw how far she'd come.

Now Gretchen turned back to Steve.

"Look, after all that I went through, you have essentially nothing to say about the letters?" she said angrily.

"No. Let me say something important," Steve said. "You aren't done with me. I worried that we were here, that we were seeing Sandy, because you were trying to make a creative, not-so-damaging split-up with me, but that's not what's been going on. You're really trying to put us back together, aren't you?"

He looked at Gretchen for an answer. God, he looked. Yes, Steve, Sandy thought. Yes.

"That's too facile," Gretchen said after a moment. "This is really complicated stuff. I realized that Bill was a transitional step. But getting back together with you? I don't know about that. I'm not there yet."

Gretchen looked at the green chair. She looked at it for almost a minute. Sandy really wanted to know what Gretchen saw there, in the chair, what the marriage looked like to her.

"Steve, if we ever get back together it has to be a completely new marriage," Gretchen said slowly.

Steve was looking at the marriage too, the marriage sitting in the green chair.

"It can't be completely new," he said. "We can't erase the past."

Gretchen turned to look at him, and there were tears in her eyes.

"You're right," she said. And they just sat there. And sat. Sandy let them. Silence was the best marriage counseling at that moment.

Finally the blue eyes clicked on, and focused on Steve.

"I'm not exactly sure what I was doing, or what we're doing now," Gretchen said. "But I do think we've been learning a lot. You know, Steve, I used to be scared of you. I was. Like giving you those letters? I never would have done it, because I would have been scared you'd hit the roof. Now? Hit it all you want. It doesn't matter."

"Sure it does," Sandy said.

"No, not really," Gretchen said.

"You know he's not going to hit the roof," Sandy said. "That's why it doesn't matter."

"Not now he won't, because you're here," Gretchen said.

"No," Sandy said. "He's just not going to hit the roof. He would have been on your doorstep when he finished reading the letters. He would have been in the street. He would have been wild. Was he?"

Gretchen looked at Steve, then back at Sandy.

"No, he wasn't," Gretchen said. "I almost called him.

He'd had the letters for a couple of days. Why hadn't I heard a reaction?"

Sandy smiled. Steve, you can be a son of a bitch, she thought.

"But I didn't call him on it, and I didn't call him," Gretchen said. "I knew he was showing me how mature he'd become."

"You know, Gretchen, there are a lot of people, they shoot each other over stuff like this," Sandy said. "Novels get written."

"Well, that's not Steve," Gretchen said. "But he should have called me."

Suddenly, she whirled around to face Steve.

"Why didn't you call me when you finished reading the letters?" she said.

"I went sort of numb," Steve said. "I could see how much I hurt you. But I could also see that, at first, you fell madly for Bill. That just shook me to the core. I couldn't call you while I was absorbing that. You had fallen in love with someone else."

Gretchen nodded. He had said something she understood.

"Me too," she said. "I read my letters before I gave them to you. It shook me to my core too. I was in love with this guy? And then I came out of it, slowly, like coming up for air. And I look back and think, What happened to me? I could have ruined my whole life with that guy. But I blame you for that. In the end, thank God, I got lucky and there were no lasting repercussions."

Sure there are, Sandy thought, but they're good ones. And Bill isn't the devil. And you do care for him. And Steve understands that. He read the letters. Neither of you can erase them.

"So now there is another issue," Sandy said. "Steve has read all the letters. What are you going to do with them?"

"I said I'd send my letters back to Bill," Gretchen said.

Everything stopped for a second. They looked at one another, more as conspirators than counselor and clients. Finally . . .

"You're kidding me," Sandy said.

"Well, I did promise that," Gretchen said. "But I think I'll burn them."

"Good idea," Sandy said.

"Can we back up to the letters before Gretchen burns them?" Steve said. "I was angry about one thing I read. I didn't appreciate the fact that Bill kept telling you to divorce me."

"But I didn't divorce you," Gretchen said.

"And I appreciate that," Steve said.

"At least not yet," Gretchen said.

Steve nodded.

"Not yet," he said. "If we ever get back together, I intend to appreciate the fact that you didn't divorce me on each and every day. I intend to work hard to make sure you don't ever divorce me."

He leaned toward her.

"Anyway, I have an idea. I want to push the boundaries." He paused again. "This is harder than I thought." He gathered himself together. "What have we been doing here, all these months? What does it lead up to?"

He let the question hang.

"I want to go back to the weekend alone together that I talked about. I want you to go away with me for a weekend without the kids," he said.

"Without Sandy?" Gretchen said.

"That's funny, but yes, without Sandy," Steve said.

Gretchen looked at him, amused.

"Please," Steve said.

He had gotten it right, Sandy thought. "Please." Or down on his knees. Or I beg you. Or something. But in the truest sense he had been right the first time, when he said it the most honest way and told Gretchen what he wanted. That was an issue Steve had problems with and would continue to have problems with in the future, telling her what he really wanted instead of what he thought she wanted.

Steve settled back in his chair. Now he seemed comfortable in it.

"I don't know what I think about that," Gretchen said. "I'd like to know what Sandy thinks, though."

You know what you think, Sandy thought.

"What do you see now, looking at Steve?" Sandy asked.

Gretchen looked hard at Steve. She looked at him for a full thirty seconds. Look at him . . .

"I see a little boy," Gretchen said. Seriously. Affectionately. Kindly. Lovingly.

It was what Sandy saw too, now, looking at Steve, the little boy in him. The macho patina had been polished off, the bluster, the false confidence. Now he just stared wide-eyed in wonder at the complexity of the world as it existed in Gretchen.

"Okay, Steve," Gretchen said finally. "We'll go away for a weekend. When?"

"I would suggest next weekend," Sandy said.

29.

It wasn't as if Sandy never learned anything of value from Heidi. Actually, knowing accounting had proved useful. Another thing that Heidi taught Sandy was that once the deal is done, shut up. Anything you add can only screw things up. So when you close a deal, wave and get out of the office.

By analogy, Sandy thought: They should go away as soon as they can. Before something can change their minds. Before Gabrielle throws a fit. Whatever. Get them to the beach as soon as you can. Even if you have to drive them.

That's what Heidi would have done.

30.

Sandy was cleaning up her desk, paying her bills, organizing her notes. She had a desk at home, but it was easier for her to concentrate in the office where she held sessions with clients. Sitting at the desk, she had her back to the chairs that she and her clients used, as well as to the green chair, the one she kept for the marriage.

Although she was the only one in the office, Sandy had an uneasy feeling of being watched. She turned around. Of course there was nothing there, but as she looked over toward the green chair, she felt the marriage looking at her impatiently.

"Oh, come on," Sandy said to the empty chair. The marriage was excited about the weekend ahead. And the marriage was worried about it too.

Is it my job to go away for the weekend with them, and to make sure that everything goes well? Sandy thought. It is not. I can't tell them that they have to be together. They have to come to that conclusion for themselves, if indeed they come to that conclusion.

All I can do is give them some skills so they can create and maintain a meaningful relationship.

My work begins and ends in this office.

"Oh, stop it," Sandy said out loud to the marriage.

The truth was that Sandy did wish she could go away for the weekend with them. She wanted their marriage to succeed. She had never been a neutral marriage counselor.

She knew that Steve was smart, and competent, but she worried about his ability to empathize with Gretchen. Yes, he had been learning and had made progress, but Sandy had her doubts.

She wished she'd had a session alone with Steve before they went away for the weekend, that she'd had a chance to go over his game plan. Did he even have a game plan? Perhaps he thought it would be contrived to have one. Maybe he just intended to wing it. He probably did.

The marriage was shaking its head.

"What do you want?" Sandy said.

Of course she knew exactly what the marriage wanted. It pushed her down the slippery slope. If you knew that you wanted the marriage to succeed, what was the point of paying lip service to the idea of the neutrality of the marriage counselor? What was the point of a marriage counselor? It had to be fixing the marriage. She spoke for the marriage.

Sandy picked up the phone on her desk, held it. She looked at it. She looked at the green chair, where the marriage waited, expectantly. Okay, she thought, I'll speak for you. She dialed. It rang once, twice, three times.

"Hello," Steve said. "Sandy?" Reading her name on his phone's face, she guessed.

"Yes," Sandy said. "Do you have a minute?"

"I do," Steve said.

"So this weekend with Gretchen?" Sandy said. "Do you have any plans for it?"

"Of course," Steve said. "I have a reservation for dinner Friday at this kind of neat place in Inverness. I think Gretchen will like it. The house I've rented is pretty cool, right on the beach in Stinson. The second night, I thought I'd cook. I'm hoping to impress Gretchen that I've actually learned how to cook. I'm bringing amazing food. And my parents are watching the kids. Gretchen is happy with that."

Was he planning on cooking Italian? Sandy let it slide.

Not a bad plan, but this is all stuff you had to do, Sandy thought. Where was the romance?

"Do you have a present?" Sandy said.

"A present?" Steve said. "Why would I have a present? What kind of present?"

"A present for Gretchen," Sandy said anxiously. "Aren't you going to do something special?"

Was he crazy?

"Of course I have a present," Steve said. "I'm sorry, I just couldn't resist leading you on."

"Don't do that with Gretchen this weekend," Sandy said.

"I won't," Steve said.

"What is it?" Sandy said.

"What is what?" Steve said.

"The present!" Sandy said. Exasperated.

Just don't give Gretchen flowers, she thought. Don't buy her anything, for God's sake. But she remembered Steve's Valentine's Day present. There was hope.

"I made Gretchen a book," Steve said. "It's taken me all week. It has the best of the notes we wrote to each other our first year together. We were pretty much madly in love. I also did some watercolors to go with the notes. One is a map of our college campus, showing the places that were important to us, like the Pamplona, a coffee shop we hung out at."

"Steve, that's great," Sandy said.

"You don't trust me, do you?" Steve said.

"Nope," Sandy said honestly.

"So do you think there's a chance that this will all work out in the end?" Steve asked.

"What do you think?" Sandy said.

"You're the marriage counselor," Steve said. "The first time I asked you, you said there was a one in a thousand chance Gretchen and I would get back together."

"I didn't know you very well back then," Sandy said. "I never should have said that to you. I'm not even sure I said it."

"Oh," Steve said. "I promise you that you did say it. It is seared into my brain. But I'm glad you did say it. It really shocked me. Blew me up. From that time on, I saw everything differently."

There was a little catch in his voice.

"I wish you were coming with us," Steve said. "Just in case we need you. I'm going to pretend you're there."

"You don't have to pretend," Sandy said. "If this work we've done is worth anything, then I'll be there. Look for me."

"You're a very peculiar marriage counselor, you know that?"

"You don't know the half of it," Sandy said. "I've been sitting in my office talking to your marriage."

Now there was a catch in her voice.

Steve laughed.

"What does the marriage say about this weekend?" Steve asked.

"The marriage thinks that Gretchen would not have agreed to go away for the weekend unless she intended to get back together with you," Sandy said.

"I wondered if that might not be true," Steve said.

"That doesn't mean you couldn't blow it all up," Sandy said.

But Sandy had high hopes. She thought Gretchen had the matter in hand. Gretchen wouldn't let Steve blow it up.

Steve said: "Are you going to call Gretchen too?"

"I have to ask the marriage," Sandy said. "But I don't think so. Bye!"

She hung up, looked at the green chair, smiled.

"Satisfied?" she asked.

The marriage smiled back.

31.

Steve was elated. Somehow it had worked, he was living with Gretchen again: the romantic weekend, the walks on the beach, the serious talks, and driving back home over the soft hills as the sun set. Gretchen saying they should live together again. Steve asking when. And Gretchen saying now, right now, you need to come home to me.

What could be more romantic than that?

Sandy looked at Gretchen. Oh, Gretchen, Sandy thought, tell him what happened.

"I'm so grateful to you," Steve said to Sandy. "You got us to this point. You got us back together."

Sandy didn't reply. She looked at Gretchen. Gretchen didn't say anything. No one said anything. Well, Sandy was the marriage counselor.

"So why now?" Sandy said, looking at Gretchen. "Why did you want to get back together now?"

"It felt like the right time," Gretchen said.

"It?" Sandy said. "Do you mean the weekend? The drive home? The sunset over the mountain? Or now after ten months living apart it felt like the right time because . . . ?"

"It was time," Gretchen said. "I had a feeling that swept through me on the drive home."

"Come on," Sandy said. "I'll admit that once in a while you have feelings that sweep you off your feet. But not very often. You've got to be extremely miserable for that to happen. And you weren't this weekend. Why did you ask Steve to come back?"

"Because I love him," Gretchen said, slowly, quietly.

"I agree, you love him," Sandy said. "You've loved him since that English class where he explained the Elizabethan poets, even though he was a jock from California. You even loved him when he wouldn't go back to the Snyders' farm, and when he drove the big Mercedes and thought he was God. But you didn't ask him to come live with you yesterday because you loved him."

"You're right," Gretchen said. "But I appreciated the romantic feelings that went into making the book he gave me."

She looked over at Steve.

"Do you see what Sandy's driving at?" Gretchen said.

Steve shook his head.

"Steve, I wasn't sure how much more of this you could take. How much more I could take. How long can we be apart before something happens that we didn't see, didn't count on? That splits us up forever. And I never thought it was good for the kids to be raised apart."

Gretchen shrugged her shoulders and looked at Sandy.

"But I still want all the rabbits," she said evenly. "I want every fucking bunny."

"I know you do," Sandy said. And you can get them, she thought.

Steve looked at his wife, uncomprehending. He just wasn't as swift as either of these women. But he did have other qualities.

"What rabbits?" Steve said.

"The Snyders' farm, those bunnies. Those fucking rabbits. Those goats," Gretchen said. "But let's not talk about it now. I don't want to live on a farm. I want to have an integrated life, with a partner who is a full participant."

Spoken like an English professor, Sandy thought.

"Steve," Gretchen said. She was emotional now. Leaning toward him. "I couldn't take it anymore. I just couldn't take it. There you have it. All the time we've been sitting here in Sandy's office, every single session, I've felt hollow, injured, as if life will never be right if we can't get it together. Like I will have lost an essential thing, the most important thing. The kids, the family. Yes, the marriage.

"But I *was* willing to lose all that rather than live a life that was trivial and fake, where you drove the big car and had affairs. I would rather have killed myself than that. But you have managed to actually change. A miracle."

She looked at them both, first Sandy, then Steve. And then she smiled, faintly.

"I realize I'm leaving myself out. Yes, I withdraw. I don't engage. I sit back. I'd rather analyze a novel than be a protagonist in my own life," Gretchen said, and then looked at Steve.

"Just because we're living together doesn't mean we're safe. There will come a time when you think I don't love you, and everything could implode all over again," Gretchen said. "You're going to make mistakes, Steve. So am I."

"I'm full of mistakes," Steve said. "But I won't make the same ones. I don't look at living together as we've solved our issues. It's more like we've been given a chance to make this work. Sandy will be here to help us."

Gretchen looked at Sandy.

"Are you going to be here?" Gretchen asked.

"Yes," Sandy said. "We have more work to do."

"How long will we keep coming to see you?" Gretchen said.

Gretchen had asked it, but it was a classic Steve question, trying to put precise values on impossible-to-answer questions.

"As long as it takes," Sandy said. "Maybe another year."

Gretchen leaned forward.

"Once we've stopped seeing you regularly, will we be able to call on you for help if we need it, if we get into trouble?" Gretchen asked.

"Of course," Sandy said.

"Long-term?" Gretchen asked.

Long-term? Where did that come from? What did Gretchen want?

Damn it, Sandy thought. She could feel her eyes going soft. She couldn't stop it.

She realized what Gretchen wanted. A burst of love swept through her. What marriage counselor can remain impartial?

Gretchen had tears at the corners of her blue eyes, which made them sparkle in the afternoon light.

Oh, honey, if only I could make you see how cool you are, how much power you have, Sandy thought.

"I'm good for the long term," Sandy said. "I'm good with forever."

Acknowledgments

I thank my wife, Emilie Osborn, and my editor, Jonathan Galassi.